onto the Pampered

home page, written

drawings of dogs.

until I started read–

> *How do you know you can count on the people looking after your dog? If you are leaving your pet with young, inexperienced caretakers, you have good reason to worry. That's why Pampered Puppy offers something new to Roxbury Park: trained professionals to care for your pet. At Pampered Puppy Doggy Day Care we offer you the peace of mind that only comes with qualified professionals! And that's the best deal out there!*

My stomach was boiling as I read it a second time. This was a clear attack on our Dog Club!

Roxbury Park • Dog Club

Roxbury Park Dog Club

TOP DOG

DAPHNE MAPLE

HARPER

An Imprint of HarperCollinsPublishers

Roxbury Park Dog Club#3: Top Dog

Text by Daphne Maple, copyright © 2016 by HarperCollins Publishers

Illustrations by Annabelle Metayer, copyright © 2016

by HarperCollins Publishers

www.harpercollinschildrens.com

Library of Congress Cataloging-in-Publication Data

Maple, Daphne.

   Top Dog / Daphne Maple.

   Roxbury Park Dog Club ; #3

   First edition.

       pages   cm

ISBN 978-0-06-232771-0 (pbk.)

PZ.1.M3696 All 2016   2015018265

Summary: "As Taylor deals with a bully at school, the Dog Club faces a new problem—competition, in the form of an upscale doggy daycare service that seems determined to put the Dog Club out of business"— Provided by publisher.

   1. Dogs—Fiction. 2. Clubs—Fiction. 3. Animal shelters—Fiction. 4. Interpersonal relations—Fiction. 5. African Americans—Fiction. [Fic]

Typography by Jenna Stempel

16 17 18 19 20 OPM 10 9 8 7 6 5 4 3 2 1

First Edition

For Erica

1

"See you tomorrow, Taylor," my friend Rachel said as we passed in the hall after the final bell. People streamed by as I waved to her and then turned toward my locker alcove and began to twirl my lock.

In some ways I was still getting used to Roxbury Park Middle School. Well, everyone in my class was, really, since it was our first year of middle school. But it was also my first year living in Roxbury Park and it still amazed me how fast it had become home. I'd lived my whole life in Greensboro, North Carolina, and when my dad announced we were moving to Illinois so he could work with an old law school friend at her firm, I cried for days. I was sure my life was over. But fast-forward two months and I had a whole new life that I loved just as much as my old one, maybe even more. Roxbury Park was a pretty, friendly town; I had two fabulous best friends; and I was a proud founding member of the Roxbury Park Dog Club. What more could a girl ask for?

"Nice shirt," someone sneered behind me. I didn't have to turn around to know it was Brianna Chen mocking what I thought was just a basic pink T-shirt.

Okay, so there was one thing I could ask for in my new life: for Brianna Chen to stop bothering me. It had started a few weeks ago: a snippy remark here, a put-down there. I kept thinking she'd get over it and find someone else to bug, but so far no luck. If anything, it was getting worse.

I sucked in my breath and turned to face her.

Brianna was Asian, with long hair, tanned skin, and a perfect fashion sense. Today she was wearing jean capris, a shimmery black shirt, and delicate silver sandals that would have given me blisters after ten minutes.

"I guess girls still wear pink where you're from, New Girl?" Brianna asked airily. She made "New Girl" sound like a gross skin disease.

"Um, yeah," I said. I never knew how to respond to Brianna's insults. I mean, how do you defend the color pink when you don't even know what's wrong with it in the first place?

Brianna raised an eyebrow, her upper lip crinkling as though just being near my pink shirt was enough to give her hives. "You might want to get rid of it now that you live here," Brianna said, smoothing a lock of sleek black hair behind one ear. "Maybe give it to a first grader or something."

I didn't know what to say but it didn't matter because Brianna had turned on her heel and was marching away, a small smile on her face.

I looked down at my shirt, which was the cheerful color of bubble gum, and tried to promise myself that I'd still wear it, that I wouldn't let Brianna's words ruin it for me. But deep down I knew they already had and that my shirt would be staying home from now on. Which was a drag because I really liked it—my sister Jasmine gave it to me because she said this color looked good with my brown skin and black hair. But I had a lot of other shirts, and it would probably be getting too cold for T-shirts soon anyway.

"Ready to go?"

This time the voice behind me made me smile. "Sure am," I said, shutting my locker and hoisting my backpack over my shoulder. Sasha, my best friend, her brown curls popping out of her ponytail, was grinning at me as she played with a strap on her backpack.

"Let's go get Kim," she said. "She wanted to talk to Mr. Martin about the test tomorrow, so I said we'd meet her at her locker."

"Is everything okay?" I asked as we headed down the hall. Kim was our other best friend, and sometimes she struggled with school. She was one of the smartest people I knew, and a total genius with dogs, but school stuff like homework and tests took her extra long and made her really anxious. Her parents tried to help and so did her older brother, Matt, but sometimes their help turned into added pressure.

"Yeah, I think she just wanted to double-check exactly what to study," Sasha said. Her steps were light and graceful as we walked; you could tell she was a dancer just by looking at her.

"That's smart," I said as we rounded the corner and found Kim stacking books into her backpack.

"You need them all?" Sasha asked playfully.

Kim smiled, but her green eyes were serious. "Last night I forgot my science book, so I'm not taking any chances today," she said, zipping up her bag and then nearly falling over when she picked it up. "Okay, maybe I can leave a couple of things here," she said, opening it back up and putting two books in her locker. "Are we running late?"

Since school was officially over, I figured it was

okay to get out my cell phone. "We're okay," I said after I looked at it. "We don't have to be at the shelter for another twenty minutes."

"That's plenty of time for our pickups," Sasha said as we walked out of the building into the sunny day. The air smelled crisp, like falling leaves and freshly mowed grass.

"I'm getting Humphrey and Popsicle, right?" Kim confirmed.

Sasha, who was in charge of our Dog Club scheduling, as well as managing our client list and handling calls from new customers, nodded. "Yes, and Taylor's getting Gus, and I'm picking up Coco and Mr. S." She was beaming as she said the last name, and who could blame her? Mr. Smashmouth had been one of the dogs at the Roxbury Park Shelter where Sasha, Kim, and I were doing our year-long volunteer assignments, a requirement of seventh grade. We loved the shelter and all the dogs there, but Sasha had made a special connection to Mr. S, a fluffy white Cavachon who was nearly blind—not that you'd know it from the way he played fetch and could sniff out a dog treat from a mile away! We were all thrilled when Sasha's mom, who is a total neat freak, finally gave in and made Sasha's dream come true by adopting Mr. S. And of course he still came to Dog Club every week, to play with all his buddies at the shelter.

"See you guys in five," Kim said. We'd reached the corner of Market Street and were separating to pick up our dogs. Kim headed down Market, Sasha turned on Grove, and I went the opposite way, toward Gus's house.

Walking the dogs to club meetings was one of the services we'd come up with after Kim had the amazing idea to start the club in the first place. The shelter was having money problems, and Kim's neighbors, the Cronins, couldn't find an affordable dog walker for their sweet basset hound, Humphrey, who needed an afternoon walk when they were at work. Two very different problems, but Kim came up with a single solution to both: the Roxbury Park Dog Club. Owners could drop their dogs off for two hours of fun and exercise at the shelter, or for an extra fee we'd pick up the dogs and walk them over ourselves. The dogs got to play, the shelter got the money it needed, and we got to hang out with dogs two days a week. It was a total win for everyone!

I slipped the key into the lock at Gus's house and heard him pad into the entry hall, panting happily.

"Hi there, sweet pea," I cooed, rubbing his soft head once I was in. Gus was a chocolate brown Lab with a face that looked like he was always smiling. I snapped his leash onto his collar and headed out.

There was a slight wind that rustled through my braids as we walked. I'd just gotten them done last weekend, with gold and silver beads at the ends. Good thing I hadn't gotten pink since I only had my hair done every few months.

Gus pranced happily at my side, clearly pleased to be out. There was a time when we picked up our dogs and then met at the town dog park so the dogs could play a bit before going to the shelter. It made for a calmer start to the afternoon, especially when we'd had Sierra, a big German shepherd mix who was super high energy. Unfortunately nothing we did helped her settle down enough to play well with the other dogs and we'd finally realized that she wasn't a good fit for our club. Her owners had been understanding, and the whole thing taught us a lot about what kinds of dogs we could handle.

The club had had other growing pains too, like when we took care of a well-groomed poodle named Clarabelle, whose owner did not want her pristine coat getting a spot of dirt on it. Of course we found this out on a wet day when the dogs were out playing in the mud, and Clarabelle's owner was not pleased. That was when we came up with our blog. We posted about what the dogs did every day so potential clients would know exactly what they were signing up for. Kim wrote each post and I provided the pictures. Photography was my thing, the way Sasha had dance and Kim was the dog whisperer.

As we headed down Main Street, passing the Rox, the diner Kim's family owned, Bundt Cake Bakery, and Nimsey's Crafts, Gus picked up his pace. We were getting close to the shelter and he knew it. Now that the dogs were used to the shelter routine, we didn't have to stop by the dog park. We just went straight to the shelter, unless we were bringing a new dog for the first time.

A moment later we were walking into the shelter, which smelled of clean fur and pine floor wax, Gus dancing in excitement as I unsnapped his leash so he could go run with his friends. Kim, Humphrey, and Popsicle had already arrived, and Tim, one of the two high school students who volunteered at the shelter, waved when he saw me.

"How's it going, Taylor?" Caley, the other high school volunteer, asked, brushing her red hair out of her face. She was into drama and sometimes practiced her lines on the dogs, who seemed to especially like Shakespeare.

"Good, thanks," I said, heading to Alice's office to set down my school stuff so I could start to play with the dogs.

Alice, who ran the shelter, was a relaxed, easygoing boss. When I walked in I realized I was interrupting a meeting, but Alice just smiled at me. "Taylor, these are the Wongs," she said, gesturing to the young couple sitting on the sofa across from her desk. "They're interested in adopting a dog."

"Terrific," I said. "You'll have a hard time choosing though—they're all awesome."

Ms. Wong smiled, the corners of her eyes crinkling. "We're excited to meet them."

Alice stood up and I saw she was wearing a T-shirt printed with the words "All you need is love . . . and a dog." "Taylor can take you out to meet everyone," she said. Just then Oscar, a fluffy gray cat, came in and hopped up onto Alice's desk. She gave his head an affectionate rub.

"If you want a cat who thinks he's a dog, Oscar is

your guy," I said, and the Wongs laughed. I led them into the main room, a big open space strewn with dog toys. One side of the room had cozy cages where the dogs slept and went if they needed a little alone time. The other wall had the bathroom and food room, as well as shelves for toys and supplies. Out back was a large fenced-in yard where we often played with the dogs.

"First meet Boxer and Lily," I said, taking the Wongs over to Tim, who was playing fetch with the two dogs.

Lily, a tan mutt, had the red rubber ball in her mouth, and Boxer, who was of course a boxer, was running after her. Lily happily deposited the soggy ball at Tim's feet and he held it out to Mr. Wong. "Want to give it a try?" he asked.

Mr. Wong was wearing a fancy-looking suit but he gamely took the ball and threw it for Boxer and Lily, who flew after it.

Kim was tossing a tennis ball for Hattie and Popsicle, so I took the Wongs over to her next. "This is Hattie,"

I said, resting a hand on the puppy's back. She was a sheepdog who used to suffer from shyness but lately had been coming out of her shell, mostly thanks to Kim and her magical way with dogs. "And this is Popsicle." I gestured to the black and white puppy. "She's a former shelter dog, here for the Dog Club, so she's not available for adoption."

"This girl is though," Kim said as Gracie, a cream-colored mutt, came over to play. She had just arrived at the shelter a few weeks ago and was still getting used to things. Sure enough, she shied away from the Wongs, since they were strangers, but Hattie went up to say hi, cautiously smelling Ms. Wong's hand when she held it out and then giving her a lick. Ms. Wong seemed to melt before my eyes as she gazed down at Hattie. Cute dogs will do that to you!

Just then the door opened and Mr. S and Coco, a big black and brown dog, burst through the door, followed by a pink-cheeked Sasha.

"More club dogs," I said to the Wongs, but they

were so busy petting Hattie that they barely heard.

Coco rushed to greet Boxer and Lily while Mr. S bounded over to Humphrey. The Cronins had adopted Popsicle after she and Humphrey bonded. Humphrey, who had been napping in the corner, got to his feet to greet his friend. They touched noses and I pulled out my camera to capture the sweet exchange. Then I looked around the shelter and snapped a few more pics: Caley on the floor rubbing Gus's tummy, Kim snuggling with Gracie and Popsicle, Sasha squealing as Lily ran up and give her a big kiss, Tim playing tug-of-war with Boxer and Lily. I loved being behind the camera lens, catching and saving these moments forever.

Mr. S came up and pressed his warm little body against my leg to say hi. I put my camera down so I could pick him up. I liked taking pictures but I liked cuddling with the dogs too! That hadn't always been true though. I'd signed up to do my volunteer assignment at the dog shelter because I wanted to be with Sasha. We'd spent our vacation together before my family moved to Roxbury Park and she was the only person I knew in town. Plus we'd hit it off right away, so hanging out with her every day after school sounded great to me. Kim wasn't that happy to have me moving in on her best friend of seven years though, and I wasn't that happy at the shelter—the big dogs made me nervous. But Kim figured that out pretty fast, and being the awesome person and amazing dog whisperer she is, she helped me out. In no time at all I was loving my time with the big dogs, and Kim and I were on the fast track to becoming best friends too.

"Who's a sweetie pie?" I asked Mr. S, picking him up and tucking him under my chin. He rewarded me with a kiss on the cheek. "Yes, you," I told him, laughing. "Your dog is the best," I told Sasha, who was walking over, a green Frisbee in hand.

"I know," Sasha said, beaming at the little dog, who began to wriggle in delight when he heard his new owner. "I'm lucky."

I set Mr. S down so he could play. "He's pretty lucky

too," I said as Sasha sent the Frisbee whizzing across the room. Mr. S, Lily, and Boxer sprinted after it.

"Want to take these guys outside?" Tim asked, coming over. His black hair was sticking out all over the place after his fun with Boxer and Lily.

"Sounds good," I said, and Sasha nodded. The three of us and Kim headed out back, Lily, Boxer, Popsicle, Mr. S, Coco, and Gus following.

"I'll stay here," Caley said, walking over to the Wongs, who were still playing fetch with Hattie. Humphrey was back to dozing in his corner, but Gracie had joined Hattie and the two of them were running after the bone-shaped toy Mr. Wong was throwing for them.

The dogs flew down the steps of the back porch and out into the grassy yard, which had worn patches from past dog playtimes. Tim charged after them and began a spirited game of fetch with Lily. Boxer frisked at Sasha's feet until she tossed the Frisbee. He took off after it, followed by Mr. S and Coco.

Kim looked at me. "Dog tag with Popsicle and Gus?" she asked. Dog tag was a game we'd invented. It started with one of us throwing a ball to the dogs and then running. The dogs would chase us with the ball, and whoever they caught first was "it" and had to throw the ball next.

"You're on," I told her, scooping up a tennis ball from the toy box on the porch and heaving it across the yard. It bounced off the big oak tree, and Popsicle and Gus raced after it. Kim and I ran in opposite directions. Popsicle got to the ball first, picked it up in her mouth, and ran to me. I dashed to Kim, who ran for the far fence, laughing. Soon we were all breathless, people and dogs alike, and all having a pretty great time.

It seemed like only five minutes had passed when Caley appeared at the door and waved us in. "Owners are starting to arrive," she called.

We trooped up the steps. My pink T-shirt was now sweaty but my whole body felt loose and energized, the best feeling ever after sitting all day in school.

"We should create a Dog Club workout," Sasha said, following me up the steps. "People would get into great shape and the dogs would get all the exercise they need."

"Sounds like a plan," Kim said. Her face was happy and relaxed the way it always was around the dogs.

Gus squeezed in front of me and ran to greet his owner, Mrs. Washington. She was wearing a pencil skirt and fitted blazer but still managed to get down and give him a big hug. "I missed you too," she said as he gave her a sloppy kiss on the side of her face.

I reached for my camera and snapped the photo, then turned and got another one of Mr. Cronin bending down to greet Humphrey, who had finally gotten up from his nap, and Popsicle. He was beaming down at his dogs while both looked up at him, their eyes filled with love. It was the perfect shot.

Soon all the club dogs except for Mr. S had been picked up. We gave final hugs to the shelter dogs, waved to Alice, Tim, and Caley, and left, Mr. S snuggled in Sasha's arms.

"Are you going to carry him all the way?" Kim asked, her eyes twinkling.

"I might," Sasha said, planting a loud kiss on the top of his fuzzy head.

A cool breeze blew as we started walking. Kim and Sasha lived down the street from each other, while my house was just a few blocks away.

Sasha was checking her phone.

"Any new messages from potential clients?" Kim asked. Alice forwarded all Dog Club voice mails to Sasha's phone.

Sasha shook her head. "No, and no messages in the Dog Club email in-box either," she said.

Kim twisted a lock of hair, a sign she was worried about something. "I think we need a few new clients," she said. "Now that Sierra's gone, we don't have that many regular dogs coming to the club."

"We have great word of mouth," Sasha said. "The clients we have love us, and I know they're spreading the word. I'm sure we'll have some new people signing up soon."

I nodded. "Remember how Mrs. Washington said she was telling her neighbor about us," I said to Kim, who was prone to stressing about things before they were a real problem. "I bet we'll hear from her this week and maybe some other people too."

Kim let out a sigh and then smiled. "I'm sure you guys are right," she said.

We'd reached the corner of Spring Street. "See you tomorrow," I said.

My friends waved and we all headed home.

2

The smell of Jasmine's world-famous (or at least family-famous) Southern fried chicken greeted me when I walked in the door.

"Dinner's almost ready," she said after I'd dropped my stuff in the front hall and arrived in the kitchen. It was a cheerful room with yellow walls, big windows, and a breakfast bar where we ate in the morning and sometimes for lunch on weekends. My dad insisted on dinners in the dining room though; he called it our civilized meal of the day.

"I'll set the table," I said, remembering it was my night and opening the drawer in the wooden island that held our big collection of silverware.

"Great," she said, drizzling dressing onto the salad she'd made. "Dad should be home any minute."

My dad worked long hours at Sasha's mom's law firm, so my sisters and I were in charge of dinner and cleaning during the week. My dad made up for it on weekends, when he'd get the barbecue going and grill ribs and pulled pork like back home.

"How was your day?" my sister Tasha asked as she walked in. She and Jasmine were twins, though they had always been pretty easy to tell apart, even before Tasha chopped off all her hair into a short Afro a few months ago. Tasha wanted to be a social worker, so she always talked about feelings and "social dynamic." Jasmine, who wore her hair in braids like mine, was on the fast track to become a doctor, so she always had her nose in a biology book and she treated her cooking nights as carefully as a surgeon. Which meant every-thing she made was pretty delicious.

I was about to tell Tash about my day when a loud, crabby voice made us all turn in alarm.

Coming into the kitchen, her face in a fierce frown, was Anna, the sister who was a royal pain. Okay, she was also a math genius and the one who organized everything around the house, like the cooking schedule and the laundry. But it seemed like her main job was giving me a hard time. And sure enough, it was me she was glaring at.

"Who did this?" she demanded, holding up some scraps of paper.

"I don't know," I said, shrugging and going back to the silverware.

"Someone cut up *Your Roxbury Park* before I had a chance to read it," Anna snapped. "And I'm pretty sure I know exactly who that someone is."

Your Roxbury Park was the Sunday magazine section of the local paper, *The Roxbury Park Gazette*. Everyone in town loved *Your Roxbury Park* because it featured fun stories from local families and businesses, things that made everyone feel good about our town.

And I actually *had* been the one to cut it up.

"I needed some pictures for an art collage," I told Anna as I brushed by, a bunch of forks in hand.

"You can't cut up the paper before everyone in the family has a chance to read it," she snapped, following me into the dining room, where I began putting the silver out on the big pecan-wood table that my parents had gotten for a wedding present. It was covered with blue striped placemats and matching napkins that my grandmother made for us.

"It's Tuesday," I pointed out calmly. Anna hated when I talked to her like she was four instead of four-teen.

"Thanks, I'm aware of what day it is," she said in a biting tone. "What's your point?"

"My point is that the paper came out on Sunday so you've had days to read it," I said, heading back to the kitchen for drinks. In fairness, I had cut up the paper on Sunday night, but since Anna hadn't discovered it until now, there was no reason to admit this.

"I had a big math test to study for," Anna snapped. "I didn't have time to read the paper until today."

I shrugged as I pulled out water glasses and began to fill them.

"You're such a brat," Anna snapped, knowing how much I hated that word.

"It's not my fault you waited until Tuesday to read the Sunday paper," I said between clenched teeth. "And don't call me that."

"You have to check with everyone in the house before you damage family property," Anna said righteously.

"The newspaper is not family property," I snapped, my calm replaced by anger that burned hot in my belly. Which was how I always seemed to feel after talking to Anna for more than five minutes. "It's just paper and we get a new one every day. It's not like I cut up the living room curtains."

"Let's try to work this out together," Tasha said, ever the peacemaker.

"Don't practice your psych homework on us," Anna said, rolling her eyes.

"Don't be mean to Tash," I said, though I kind of secretly agreed with Anna. It was irritating when Tasha pretended to be the family therapist. But I wasn't going to take Anna's side now, not after she called me a brat.

Tasha threw up her hands. "Whatever," she said.

"You have to promise you won't cut up the paper again," Anna told me, crossing her arms over her chest like she was some kind of army drill sergeant. Which would be a really good career choice for her.

"No," I said, infuriated at how she always tried to boss me around. "You can't tell me what to do!"

"Then I'm telling Dad!" Anna shouted back.

"Telling Dad what?" We'd been so loud that neither of us had heard my dad come in. Now he was stand-ing in the doorway, still in his blue work suit, looking tiredly between me and Anna.

"Nothing, Daddy," Anna said quickly.

"Everything's fine," I added.

We girls didn't like to make things hard for our dad We knew it was tough for him raising four girls on his own, ever since Mom had died six years ago, and we didn't want to make it any tougher. I really did try to get along with my sisters; it was just that Anna made it impossible.

"It seems like the two of you have been bickering a lot lately," he said.

"That's the truth," Tasha muttered as she began collecting the water glasses I'd filled to take out to the table.

"Sorry," I said, feeling bad.

"We'll try to do better," Anna added.

As soon as Dad had headed upstairs to change, I shot Anna a furious look. "That was your fault," I whispered angrily.

"Actually it was yours," she said frostily, then

sashayed out of the kitchen, getting in the last word like always.

I finished filling up glasses, seething as I poured. Being the littlest sister was a drag, but being Anna's little sister was the worst.

3

"Good girl," I told Gracie as she carefully deposited a chewed-up teddy bear at my feet. For some reason this was her toy of choice, and she always had it to herself since the other dogs preferred fetching balls. I grabbed the bear and tossed it across the shelter, and Gracie went skittering after it.

Rain pattered gently on the roof and windows of the shelter. Usually I preferred sunny days to rainy ones, but there was something cozy about being warm and playing with dogs while the rain came down. The weather seemed to have a calming effect on the dogs too. They were playing, of course, but the energy in the room was lower than usual. Or maybe it was just me. Brianna had been talking about me as we walked out of school. I couldn't hear what she was saying and I didn't really know the girls she was with, so it shouldn't have mattered. But the way her eyes glinted as she looked at me, lowering her voice when I passed, made me feel like I'd swallowed something hard and sharp. It was still gnawing at me, though Gracie coming up with her bear and wagging her tail at me helped. Kim coming over and putting an arm around me helped too.

"Are you okay?" she asked.

"Yeah," I said, trying to smile. I hadn't told my friends about the stuff with Brianna. I was still hoping it would just go away on its own.

She gave my shoulders a squeeze. "Okay," she said. She was about to say more when the door of the shelter opened and Tim and Caley came in. They'd been walking under a big black umbrella, which Tim left in the entryway, and their shoes made wet, squelching noises on the floor.

It was weird that Caley and Tim were late; usually they got here before us because the high school let out fifteen minutes earlier. As they came in, I realized both of them were frowning. Clearly something was up.

"Have you guys seen this?" Caley asked, holding out a soggy but colorful piece of paper.

Sasha took it from her, and Kim and I gathered around so we could read it together.

Pampered Puppy was at the top of the page. Pampered Puppy was the fancy grooming place on Main Street that also sold designer collars and expensive dog toys. We'd actually hung flyers there when we were starting the club. But now it looked like they were starting a club of their own. My stomach tightened as I read on.

*Does your dog spend lonely hours at home
while you're at work? Let us help! Our professional,
trained staff will pamper a select group of dogs who
play well together, enjoying companionship, fun,
and lots of exercise while you're at the office. You
can check up on your pet anytime—our Doggy Day
Care webcams stream live so you don't have to miss
a second of your dog's good time at our new, top-of-
the-line doggy care center.*

My stomach was now knotted up as I looked at the
photo on the bottom of the page. Even on a water-
stained piece of paper, you could see how fancy their
care center was: huge with a gleaming wooden floor,
brand-new dog toys, and smiling staff. Adult staff.

"Uh-oh," Kim said.

"Yeah," Tim said with a sigh. "That's what we said
too."

"This place looks so fancy," Sasha said, her eyes still
on the page. "A lot of dog owners are really going to
like that."

"Plus their staff is trained," Kim said glumly. "And they're grown-ups, not just kids like us."

"I consider myself to be very mature," Caley said, then sighed. "But I see your point."

"And they have a webcam," I said. All of it was bad, but somehow that seemed the biggest blow. My dog photos on our blog could never compete with an actual live view of the dogs anytime an owner wanted one. And there was no way we could move Alice's computer out of her office and use the webcam on that to film our dogs; Alice was too busy working in the afternoons.

"I wish we could post photos of us with the dogs," Sasha said. "So people could see how much fun they have with us." Since the blog was public, our parents and Alice only let us post dog pictures, none of us.

"That would be great," I said with a sigh because I knew our parents and Alice were never going to change their minds on that one.

Kim put an arm around me again but I could feel how tense she was when she squeezed me.

"This is bad, you guys," Sasha said.

I looked around at our sad little group. Caley was biting her lip, Tim was running his hands through his hair, and Sasha was still staring at the flyer like it was something dangerous.

I squared my shoulders. "Come on, y'all," I said. "We can't let a little flyer get us down."

Sasha grinned. "I love it when you go Southern on us," she said.

Caley shook her head as though coming out of a trance. "Taylor's right," she said. "This isn't necessarily a problem. I mean, who knows—it could be super expensive or close in a week. We have a great business, we're getting new clients all the time, and, professional or not, we are super good at taking care of dogs."

As though he agreed, Boxer ran up to Caley and barked happily. Caley laughed and rubbed his ears.

"The families we have love our club," Sasha said, sounding slightly more optimistic. "I don't think any of them would ever leave."

But Kim was twisting her hair. "We need some new

clients though," she said. "And having competition in town will make that harder."

"The flyer says they take a select group of dogs," Tim said. "Aside from sounding snobby, that also sounds like they are only looking for a few clients. So hopefully they'll just get people whose dogs wouldn't work at our club anyway."

"Leaving everyone else for us," Caley said triumphantly.

Sasha had finally set down the flyer, and Kim was bending down to pet Hattie, who had come over for some attention. Kim's movements were relaxed and I knew she was feeling better. It seemed like we all were.

Then Sasha's phone beeped with a message. "Oh, it's from Alice," she said, looking at the screen. "She forwarded me an email."

Kim and I exchanged a happy look as Sasha read the message; it had to be a call from a possible client! Clearly things were just fine for the Roxbury Park Dog Club, no matter who else was opening a care center.

"It was Mrs. Washington's neighbors and they sounded really interested," Sasha bubbled as she stuffed her phone into her pocket. "They said they'd look at the website and then get in touch again."

"What kind of dog do they have?" Kim asked, a slight crease between her brows. I knew she was thinking of Sierra and Clarabelle and wanted to make sure the dog would be a good fit for the club.

"An older collie mix who loves to play," Sasha said.

Kim smiled. "Sounds like she'd be a great addition to the club."

Lily bounded up to us, a red ball in her mouth. Coco and Gracie were right behind her. The crisis had passed and it was time to play! Kim picked up the ball and sent it sailing across the room. Sasha began a game of tug-of-war with Hattie, and I headed over to Humphrey and Popsicle, who were in the back corner. Humphrey was clearly debating whether or not to take a nap, while Popsicle was nosing at a green chew toy.

"Let's play some catch," I said to them, picking up a

tennis ball. Both dogs took off when I threw it. It always made me smile to see Humphrey run on his short little legs, his long ears rippling. *Run* actually wasn't the right word since he moved pretty slowly, but he clearly thought he was the fastest dog in the room and seemed surprised when Popsicle reached the tennis ball first.

"You'll get it next time," I told him, deciding to throw two balls so that he'd have a chance.

"Afternoon, everyone," Alice said, coming in and shaking the rain off her umbrella. She'd gone to the post office as soon as we'd arrived. "How's it going?"

I looked at Kim and Sasha, remembering the flyer and how anxious it had made us. But now it didn't seem like that big a deal.

"Everything's great," I said firmly.

4

"It's getting late," Kim said, peering down Spring Street toward Sasha's house. We were on the corner where the three of us met up every morning so we could walk to school together. Sasha was usually the last to arrive since she was prone to forgetting things and having to run back. But she was always here by 8:15 and now it was almost 8:20. If we didn't leave in the next minute or two, we were going to be late.

"Yeah, it is," I said, looking to see if I could catch a glimpse of Sasha running to meet us. "Do you think she's sick?"

Kim shook her head. "She'd text if she wasn't coming."

"Maybe she has a dentist appointment and forgot to tell us?" I asked.

Kim bit her lip for a moment. "I guess that's possible, but she usually complains for days before the dentist because she hates having her teeth cleaned."

This was the kind of thing that Kim, as Sasha's long-time best friend, knew better than me. But it instantly made sense; Sasha had a thing about stuff getting stuck in her mouth and didn't even like lollipops.

"What should we do?" Kim asked, twisting at her hair. I knew the thought of being tardy stressed her out.

I was about to answer when my phone vibrated. I pulled it out of my pocket and saw that there was a text from Sasha. "She says to go ahead without her," I said after I'd read it. "She just got back from walking Mr. S and still has to feed him."

Kim frowned as we started walking toward school. Actually it was almost jogging since we wanted to get there before the first bell. "This isn't like Sasha," she said.

"I know," I agreed. "I mean, she forgets stuff, but this is different."

"Yeah," Kim said. "She might mess up little things but nothing big, like getting a tardy on her school record."

"It's probably hard for her to get up earlier now that she has a dog to walk before school," I said, thinking about how Sasha was always the last one up at sleepovers.

"I bet her mom's not happy," Kim said with a sigh.

I nodded knowingly. Sasha's mom was kind of a superwoman. She was raising Sasha on her own (though Sasha did see her dad in the summers when she'd go stay with him in Seattle), she ran a law firm, her house was spotless, and she always looked perfect, never a hair out of place. And needless to say, she was never, ever late.

"Maybe she'll give Sasha a ride," I said hopefully as the redbrick school building came into view. "Give her a break since she's still adjusting to being a dog owner."

"I hope so," Kim said as we dashed up the front steps.

But when Mrs. Benson took roll call in homeroom, Sasha's seat was empty.

"Watch it," Brianna snapped at me as I rounded the corner and nearly bumped into her. Although when I jumped back, I realized we were actually pretty far apart. She was just acting like I'd nearly plowed her over because that's what she always did. At least with me.

"Sorry," I said, not wanting to make a big thing of it.

"You need to look where you're going," she said disdainfully. "You're so clumsy you could really hurt someone."

I drew in a breath at that, as though she'd hit me. Which was kind of how it felt. Yes, I sometimes tripped, but everyone did; it didn't make me a klutz. Did it?

"Oh, and how's business at your little dog club?" Brianna asked, a sly smile spreading over her face.

As seemed to always be the case with Brianna, I had no idea why she was asking and no idea how to respond. "Um, fine," I said.

"Enjoy it while it lasts," Brianna said. "Because my mom's new doggy day care is going to put you guys out of business."

That news made my stomach drop. If Brianna's mom was anything like her daughter, we really were in trouble.

But Brianna wasn't done yet. "Maybe you can use the free time to take dance classes or something, so you can stop slamming into people." With that she flounced off down the hall and I heard her calling a friendly greeting to a couple of girls in our English class. Her voice was warm, not all ice and sharp edges the way it was when she talked to me.

I was standing in the hall as the girls passed and said

hi. I did my best to act normal but I was still feeling shaky. Plus something ugly was beginning to worm its way into my mind. Brianna was nice to these girls, who all had one thing in common: they were white. I didn't like to jump to conclusions but I was starting to wonder if part of Brianna's problem with me was my race. I mean, I hadn't done anything to her and we'd never really even said hello before she started making mean remarks when I passed. It was possible she didn't like something else about me, but the fact was, it was also possible that she had issues with black people. And that thought was like a cold wind blowing right through me.

"Hey, aren't you coming to lunch?" Sasha asked, coming up behind me. She'd arrived ten minutes after school began, breathless and near tears. But now she looked calm.

"Do you think I'm clumsy?" I blurted out.

"What? No, you're perfect," Sasha said.

"You're my friend, so you have to say nice things," I told her as we started walking toward the cafeteria.

"Um, actually I don't," Sasha said seriously. "You're tall and graceful and no clumsier than anyone else, I promise."

Her words made me feel a million times better. "Thanks," I said, giving her a hug.

She squeezed me back but she was frowning. "What made you ask about that anyway?"

"Oh, nothing important," I said. The encounter with Brianna still needled at me but I didn't want to think about it now.

The cafeteria smelled of boiled greens and old meat, not exactly appetizing. Sasha and I bypassed the steaming trays of hot entrees and headed to our usual station, the salad bar. Sasha threw together a spinach-and-tuna salad while I grabbed a strawberry yogurt with granola to mix in.

Once we paid for our food, we headed to our table on the back wall by the window. Kim was already there, turkey sandwich in front of her. She was chatting with our friends at the neighboring table, Naomi,

Emily, Rachel, and Dana.

"Hey, guys," Emily said as Sasha and I sat down next to Kim. "What's shaking?"

"That would be me and Dana," Sasha said with a grin. They were both in the company at their dance school, which was pretty cool; a lot of girls had tried out but only a few got in. It meant dance classes three times a week and extra performances, but Sasha always managed her busy schedule just fine. Well, she had until this morning anyway.

"How are things at the garden?" I asked as I sat down next to Kim and began peeling the foil top off my yogurt. The four of them had signed up to do their seventh-grade volunteer work at the town garden on the edge of the park. It had started as an assignment but lately they had been getting excited about the fall planting and late harvest they were doing.

"We're going to be planting winter radishes today," Rachel said enthusiastically. "Luciana says they taste great in salads."

"Sounds good," Sasha said, crunching on a snap pea. "Be sure to bring some in when they're ready." We often brought in food to share with each other.

Rachel nodded. "And how's the Dog Club?" Of course the four of them knew all about it.

Kim pressed her lips together for a second. "Good, but we could use a few new clients."

"We'll help spread the word," Naomi said. "Advertising is everything."

Dana was nodding. "Do you guys have any extra flyers? We can put a few up at the garden."

Now Kim was smiling. "That would be awesome. I think we have some extras at my house. I'll bring them tomorrow."

I remembered what Brianna had said about her mom owning Pampered Puppy and I wondered if I should mention it. But since I didn't feel like talking about Brianna, I decided to let it go for now.

"Rough morning, huh," Kim said sympathetically to Sasha, who shook her head.

"You have no idea," she said, spearing a grape tomato with her fork. "Everything that could go wrong did: my alarm didn't go off, I couldn't find Mr. S's leash, he threw up right after he ate, all over the living room rug, and my mom left early for a meeting, so she couldn't help me with any of it. Though maybe that's a good thing—I think she'd have freaked out over the puke on her favorite rug."

Sasha's mom really loved Mr. S (who wouldn't?) but she was still getting used to the messy side of owning a pet.

"Did you get it clean?" I asked. "Because I have a few tips if you need them. Last year I got grape jelly on our sofa and I learned a lot about getting out stains." Anna had told me I'd never get the stain out, so I spent the entire day researching on the internet and finally managed to get it off with vinegar and a baking soda scrub.

Sasha nodded. "Yeah. But I may be calling you soon if I keep having mornings like this one."

"It seems like the biggest problem was the alarm clock," I said. "Once you have that one fixed, at least you'll have time to deal with everything else."

"Yeah, that makes sense," Sasha said. "Though lately it seems like I don't have enough time for anything."

Kim and I exchanged a look. It wasn't like Sasha to sound so down.

But a second later she was grinning. "Oh, but I have some good news," she said. "Alice forwarded me another call from a dog owner interested in our club."

"Great," Kim said, her eyes lighting up.

"That's two calls in two days," I said, feeling happy. "We're on a roll."

"Now we just need them to sign up," Kim said.

She looked slightly anxious and I knew she was thinking about Pampered Puppy. But I was certain she had nothing to worry about; once the potential clients saw our website and how sweet our dogs were, they'd be signing up in no time.

5

"Hey, wait up," Kim called.

It was a perfect sunny day and I'd just picked up Coco and was heading toward the shelter. I turned and waited as Kim and Gus trotted up.

"Hi," I said to both of them, reaching down to pet Gus, who wriggled joyfully.

Kim rubbed Coco's ears, and the big black and brown dog panted happily.

Greetings done, we headed into town, the dogs prancing beside us.

"I can't believe how much reading we have for English tonight," Kim said with a sigh. We'd just started a nonfiction unit and were reading a biography of Eleanor Roosevelt.

"Yeah, it's a lot," I agreed. "And that book is tough going. It always puts me to sleep after about three pages."

Kim gave a lopsided grin. "I'm glad I'm not the only one," she said. "Eleanor Roosevelt seems really interesting; you'd think the book wouldn't be such a snooze."

I was about to agree when I saw something that made me draw in a sharp breath. We'd just turned onto Main Street, where there were five bright flyers stapled to the bulletin board in front of the town hall. Five flyers advertising Pampered Puppy's Doggy Day Care.

"They're everywhere," Kim said, sounding slightly in awe. Sure enough, every free space along Main Street was papered with a colorful ad for the new doggy day care. As we began walking slowly down the street, we saw that they weren't all the same flyer, the way ours were. There were a bunch of different ones—some with photos, others with cute drawings, and all of them announcing the doggy day care as the most amazing place ever.

"These flyers are so much better than ours," I said, looking at one with a picture of a smiling staff member, adult of course, playing with a Jack Russell. The photo, the font, the way it was all put together looked sleek, like something you'd see in a magazine. And pretty much the opposite of our homemade black-and-white flyers, which didn't have pictures or anything. Even the paper they were printed on was thicker and nicer than ours.

"They really are," Kim said. The corners of her mouth were turning down as she stared at them.

Coco gave a short bark. Clearly she thought we were moving too slowly.

"Let's get to the shelter," I said, picking up the pace. "We can talk about it there."

When we opened the door, we were greeted by cheerful barks from the shelter dogs as well as Daisy, who'd already been dropped off, and Popsicle, Mr. S, and Humphrey, who had already arrived with Sasha. Gus and Coco raced off to join their friends, all happy and excited. But when I looked around at Caley, Tim, and Sasha, I could tell from their glum expressions that they had seen the flyers too. Though that wasn't really surprising—you'd have to be walking through town blindfolded to miss them.

"So Pampered Puppy is serious about their doggy day care," Caley said with a sigh. Her red hair was in a bun held together with black chopsticks and she reached up to tighten it. "And they want the whole town to know."

"I know—it seems like they killed an entire forest to put all those up," Tim said, shaking his head as he bent down to scratch Humphrey's belly.

"Everyone knows about their doggy day care now for sure," Sasha said. She was on the floor cuddling Mr. S and Popsicle.

Lily came over and pressed against my leg, looking

up at me with her big brown eyes. It was as though she could tell I needed cheering up. Dogs were amazing like that. I sat down, my backpack still on, and gave her a big hug.

"What if people start calling them instead of us?" Kim fretted. "And what if our customers start going to Pampered Puppy because it's better?"

"Whoa, hold on there," Tim said, putting up a hand that Boxer, who was standing next to him, licked. "Let's not get into the what-if game."

Caley had a hand on her hip and she gave Kim a stern look. "And who said anything about them being better? Fancier, maybe, but we offer the best care around."

"And I bet we have the better price," Sasha said, suddenly sounding more cheerful.

"That's a great point," I said, my hands buried in Lily's soft fur. "We offer good care at a good rate and there's no way Pampered Puppy can say that, not when they have all those *professionals* to pay."

Everyone laughed at that.

"But we do need new clients," Kim said, her forehead creased. "Sash, have those people called you back to sign up yet?"

For a moment Sasha frowned. "No, but I bet they will."

"Me too," I said. "And remember, Rachel and those guys are going to put up some flyers for us. We're getting the word out about our club too."

That seemed to comfort Kim, who finally smiled.

Just then the door opened and we all turned to see the Wongs. "Is it okay if we come in for a bit?" Ms. Wong asked, tucking a strand of long black hair behind one ear. "We didn't call Alice but we're still planning to adopt one of the dogs and we had a few minutes to come by and see them."

"She's at a meeting," Tim said. "But come on in."

"The dogs are always happy to have friends stop by," I added, standing up and brushing Lily's fur off my shirt. I headed to Alice's office to stow my bag, then went back out into the main room, where the Wongs were already playing fetch with Hattie and Lily. Tim was still down on the floor with Humphrey, and Mr. S had come over for a tummy rub of his own. Kim was throwing a ball for Gus and Daisy, while Sasha was snuggling with Gracie.

Boxer came up to me, his favorite green Frisbee in his mouth, a glint in his eye.

"Let's get that in the air," I told him. He dropped it at my feet with a short bark, his eyes glued to the disc as I raised it up and sent it sailing across the room. Boxer flew after it.

I was still worried about Pampered Puppy; I knew we all were. But as the afternoon passed with the dogs, it was impossible not to feel cheered up. And by the time we left, worn out but happy the way only dogs can make you happy, I barely noticed the flyers covering the town.

I was thinking about them later that night though, when I was supposed to be reading the Eleanor Roosevelt biography. Naomi's words about advertising being everything were haunting me. If she was right, we were in trouble.

It had been Jasmine's night to cook and she'd baked a peach cobbler for dessert that had been delish. I set down my book, deciding that it would be easier to work more and worry less if I had some more cobbler. There was probably some whipped cream left too.

I hurried down to the kitchen but stopped in the doorway. Anna was sitting at the island, feet wrapped around her stool as she ate the last of the cobbler from the glass pie plate. The empty bowl of whipped cream sat next to it.

"Hey, I wanted that," I accused, walking in.

Anna smiled lazily, then licked her fork. "I guess you should have been faster then," she said. She had a point but she didn't need to be so smug about it.

I began pawing through the cabinet for something sweet, but nothing looked as good as fresh cobbler. "You didn't have to pig the whole thing," I grumbled at Anna, pulling out a box of chocolate chip cookies.

She was rinsing the dishes at the sink but paused to glare at me. "For your information, there wasn't much left," she said. "Probably because you pigged so much at dinner."

"I only had one serving, unlike some people," I said snidely, feeling pleased when her cheeks flushed. When she was this annoying, all I wanted to do was annoy her back, and it looked like I'd succeeded.

"At least I didn't completely inhale the whipped cream," she snapped. "You hardly left any for Dad."

Now my cheeks were burning and she was the one smiling. "I did not," I said hotly, my hands on my hips. "There was some left over, wasn't there?"

"What is going on in here?"

Anna and I both turned to see Tasha in the doorway looking just as annoyed as we were.

"Taylor came in and picked a fight," Anna said, just as I said, "Anna ate all the leftover cobbler."

"Stop yelling," Tasha said irritably, with no trace of

her social worker tone. "Some of us are trying to get homework done."

I hadn't realized Anna and I were yelling but I was kind of out of breath.

"Tell her to stop bothering me then," Anna crabbed, turning back to finish cleaning off her dishes.

"I'm not bothering anyone, I'm just trying to get a snack in my own kitchen," I said, feeling fed up with Anna.

Tasha shook her head. "You two are impossible," she said, heading back upstairs.

"You're the impossible one," Anna said, drying her hands and nearly running out so she could have the last word.

But this time I followed her. "She was talking about you!" I shouted after her.

Then I headed back to the kitchen for the cookies, which weren't cobbler but would be sweetened by the fact that I'd won this round.

6

I was glad to see Sasha waiting at the corner of Spring Street the next morning.

"Your alarm was working?" I asked as I came up. There was a chilly wind blowing and I hugged my baby-blue hoodie tight around me.

Sasha grinned. "Actually, Mr. S woke me up with kisses, which is the best wake-up ever," she said.

"Definitely," I agreed as Kim arrived. She had dark circles under her eyes and was yawning.

"Late night?" I asked her.

She nodded and rolled her eyes as we started walking. "Yeah, it took me forever to finish the reading for English."

Sasha gasped.

"It wasn't that bad," Kim said, her brows knit together. "I just went to bed a little later than usual."

"No, it's not that," Sasha said, sounding panicked. "I totally forgot to read the assignment last night, and you know Mrs. Benson will be giving us a quiz."

Kim looked at me, eyes wide. Because yes, Mrs. Benson was the queen of pop quizzes, and since we hadn't had one yesterday we were definitely getting one today. And it had been a lot of reading.

"Let's get moving," I said, starting to jog toward school. "Maybe you can read it before homeroom starts."

"It was a lot though," Sasha said anxiously. "I don't think I can finish it."

"But reading some of it is better than none," I

pointed out. "Maybe most of the questions will be from the first part or something."

"Maybe," Sasha said, but her face was tight.

"What happened?" Kim asked as we came to a stop at the corner and waited while a pickup truck drove past. "Did you forget about it or something?"

"I just, I don't know," Sasha said, chewing on her lip for a moment and then going back through her night. "I got home from dance and walked Mr. S and fed him, and then we had dinner and I helped my mom clean up. I did my math and social studies but I was so tired after that I just went to bed."

I saw Kim frown and I knew why: this was not Sasha. And failing a quiz would not be good. When we crossed the street I started running, to give her more time to read.

By the time we arrived at school Kim and I were panting, but Sasha was cool as a cucumber, probably because she was in great shape from all those dance classes.

"I'm going straight to homeroom," Sasha said, hiking her backpack over one shoulder. "I'll put my stuff away later."

"See you guys in a minute," I said, ducking into my locker alcove. The five-minute bell hadn't rung yet, so people were milling around but it wasn't super crowded. I spun my combination and then piled my stuff into my locker. As I shut the door I heard a sharp burst of laughter. Three girls were standing in the corner looking at something in a magazine, and one of the girls was Brianna. I looked away, not wanting her to catch my eye, then realized something. The two girls she was hanging out with, Kendra and Meredith, were black. I watched as Meredith read something out loud in a funny voice and Brianna clutched her arm and giggled. It wasn't like you could tell everything from one moment, but it didn't seem like Brianna had any problem at all with Kendra and Meredith being black. In fact, if anything, she looked overjoyed to be hanging out with them.

As though she could feel my gaze, Brianna glanced over and her eyes narrowed. Then she sneered and turned back to her friends, the ugly look falling away from her face as she began joking with them again.

So maybe it wasn't my race that was the problem, maybe it was just me. But why? What had I ever done to Brianna? And more importantly, what could I do to get her to leave me alone?

Saturday afternoon I walked up the steps of Sasha's silver-and-blue Victorian house and rang the bell. The three of us had sleepovers almost every weekend, and this time we were staying at Sasha's. I heard Mr. S barking excitedly and a moment later Sasha opened the door, looking frazzled.

"Hey," she said, raking a hand through her messy curls.

"Is everything okay?" I asked, bending down to pet Mr. S before following Sasha into the house.

"Yeah, I'm just kind of behind," she said. "My mom left me a list of chores and I'm only about halfway through."

"Let's finish them up then," I said, setting my

overnight bag on the steps and taking off my pink cotton jacket. It was the weekend, so I figured I was safe wearing pink. I almost forgot to slip off my black flats but then noticed Sasha was barefoot. Not surprisingly, theirs was a shoes–off house.

"You don't mind helping me out?" Sasha asked, relieved.

"Of course not," I said, putting an arm around her shoulders. "What do we need to do?"

Sasha led me to the kitchen, where there was a stack of dirty dishes in the sink with traces of syrup on them. "I'll take care of the dishes if you don't mind putting the groceries away."

I saw three reusable bags set neatly on the big island, the same kind we had at home. Sasha's mom and my dad were both environmental lawyers, so our families had big recycle bins and reusable everything. Not that I minded; my dad had explained how important it was to create less trash, plus it was no big deal to use a metal water bottle instead of buying disposable plastic ones.

I started in on the first bag, which was mostly veggies and fruit. Once I had them tucked away in the fridge, I reached into the second bag. "Oh, you guys got caramel for milk shakes tonight," I said. One of our sleepover traditions was making milk shakes with lots of fun mix-ins. Caramel was Kim's favorite.

"We also got peanut butter," Sasha said with a grin. I always tried different combos, but peanut butter and chocolate were my all-time favorites.

"Awesome," I said, pulling out vanilla cookies that we could blend in for added crunch, along with M&M's and rainbow sprinkles. "It looks like you have everything covered."

"Yeah, and the ice cream is in the freezer," Sasha said. She was done with the dishes and was drying her hands off on a red-striped hand towel. "The last thing I need to do is vacuum the living room."

"I can help with that," I said.

"Actually, the vacuum scares Mr. S, so if you wouldn't mind taking him out while I get it done, that would be awesome," she said. She had pulled the vacuum out of the hall closet and Mr. S was staring at it suspiciously.

"I can't think of anything I'd like more," I told Sasha. I grabbed one of Mr. S's rubber balls from a basket in the front hall, and a minute later we were playing a lively game of fetch in the front yard.

"Can I join you?" Kim asked, coming up the path.

Mr. S bounded over to greet her and she bent down and ruffled his ears.

"We were hoping you would," I said, tossing her the ball.

I saw that she was frowning, which was very strange for Kim—anytime she was around a dog she was usually smiling.

"What's wrong?" I asked.

She bit her lip and then shook her head. "Let's wait till we're inside with Sasha," she said. Which kind of curdled my stomach.

I watched Mr. S run after the ball Kim threw and

cheered him on when he returned with it in his mouth, wagging his tail in triumph. But it was a relief when Sasha called us in a few minutes later.

"So what's going on?" I asked Kim the second we were inside.

Sasha gave us a quizzical look.

Kim slipped off her sneakers and sighed. "Pampered Puppy made a really great video to advertise their new doggy day care," she said. "It already has a ton of views."

"Ugh," I said.

"Yeah," Kim agreed. "You guys need to see it."

"Do we have to?" Sasha asked, but she was already heading upstairs to her room.

I knew what she meant. I didn't want to see some amazing thing Pampered Puppy had created either. But if it was out there, we had to know about it.

Sasha's room was painted lavender and the comforter on her bed was a bright purple. Her bookshelf was crowded with a lot of my favorites and she had a big bulletin board filled with pictures of vacations with her mom, visits to her dad, and of course me and Kim. There were bunches of shots I'd taken at the shelter, and it normally made me happy to see them. But today all I could think about was Pampered Puppy.

Kim typed in the website and we waited while it loaded—Sasha's computer was old. A minute later a slow, sad tune began to play and the screen filled with a dog standing in a dim front hallway looking dejectedly at the door. After a moment the dog walked to the window and looked out, then let out a sigh and settled on the floor, alone in a dark, empty room. "Does your dog miss you when you're working those long hours at your job?" a sympathetic voice asked. "Do you worry about all that time alone, deprived of a companion to play with?" A moment later the melancholy tune was replaced by an upbeat jazz song and the camera panned over a huge room with polished wooden floors, bright white walls, and big windows. Fancy dog beds and toys were placed strategically, giving the perfect dash of color to the scene. "Maybe your dog would have more fun playing with us!" the voice said. Then four dogs bounded in and began to frolic about. Two smiling women walked in, both wearing T-shirts that spelled out "Pampered Puppy Doggy Day Care" in swirly letters. One began petting a dog, who jumped up to give her a big kiss. The other began playing catch with the remaining dogs. "Pampered Puppy Doggy Day Care," the voice said. "Where your dog gets the best care possible. Opening in just one week. Sign up today for our special introductory offer and get two months for the price of one!" The screen faded so that all you could see was the Pampered Puppy name and their contact info in pretty, swirly letters.

"That's bad," Sasha said, sinking down on her bed.

"Really bad," I agreed. "I can't believe they have that introductory offer. A lot of people are going to like a deal like that."

"And they open in just a few days," Kim said. She was in Sasha's desk chair, twirling a lock of hair like crazy.

I wanted to say something positive, something to cheer us up and rally us to get behind our Dog Club instead of worrying about theirs. But as the video began to play again, I couldn't find the words. Instead I just watched in silence as Pampered Puppy told the world how great it was.

7

"Big news," Alice said when the three of us and our club dogs walked into the shelter a few days later. "The Wongs are going to adopt Hattie!"

That *was* big news. It was great when a shelter dog found a home, and the Wongs seemed super nice. I knew they'd take great care of Hattie, though of course Alice would never let anyone take a dog unless they were totally qualified.

"Tim's out getting a cake," Alice said. Her eyes were

shining and she straightened her T-shirt, which was printed with dalmatians. "We're going to celebrate."

"Terrific," Kim said. She snapped Gus's leash off then went over to pat Hattie's head.

I released Coco and joined them. "You're going to have a new home, Hattie," I told her.

She looked up, and the sight of her sweet little face made my chest clench. I would miss her!

"You girls should be sure to tell the Wongs about the Dog Club," Alice said. "I bet they'll be interested."

I looked at Alice gratefully. It would be perfect if we got to have Hattie at the Dog Club. She'd have a home, but we'd still get to see her. Alice was gazing fondly at the little sheepdog, and I realized she would miss Hattie too. It must be hard to run a shelter where your job was to love the dogs but then try to find them homes. That was one of the many things that made Alice so awesome. And the Dog Club too: that was how we still got to see Popsicle every week, and now I had my fingers crossed that the Wongs would join so we'd still get to play with Hattie.

"Great idea, Alice," Sasha said. "We'll definitely tell them all about it."

Hattie gave out a bark, as though she understood, and then ran over to say hi to Mr. S. I picked up a blue rubber ball and threw it for the two of them, laughing as they dashed after it, Gus at their heels. Sasha tossed a tennis ball for Boxer, Lily, and Coco, while Kim went over to Humphrey and tried to coax him into a game of tug-of-war. Caley was snuggling on the floor with Daisy and Gracie, and Alice smiled at the scene, then headed into her office.

A few minutes later the door opened. "Cake's here," Tim called.

Alice hurried back into the big room. "Great," she said. "Let's try to set everything up so it's ready when the Wongs get here at five."

In between playing with the dogs, we put up a folding table; set out plates, napkins, and forks; and took turns guarding the cake box from the dogs, who knew something good when they smelled it.

Right at five the door opened.

"Congratulations!" We cheered as the Wongs came in. Hattie ran to greet them, along with Popsicle and Gus.

"This is quite a celebration," Mr. Wong said, looking surprised and pleased.

"There's a lot to celebrate," Alice said. "It's a wonderful thing when a dog finds a home."

"We're happy for you guys and we're happy for Hattie," I said. Kim was slicing the cake while Sasha put it on plates, which I passed around.

"This is delicious," Ms. Wong said after her first bite.

"Bundt Cake Bakery makes the best cakes," Caley said, then glanced at Kim. "But for pies the only place to go is the Rox."

Kim smiled at the mention of her family's diner.

Tim was nodding enthusiastically. "And the Rox's sweet potato fries are the best. You need to bring those in once in a while," he told Kim.

"Oh, does your family own the Rox?" Ms. Wong asked.

Kim nodded proudly.

"Those sweet potato fries really are tasty," Ms. Wong agreed. "We eat there every Friday night. Though I guess now we'll need to get home right after work for Hattie." She was looking across the room to where Hattie was now romping with Gracie and Gus.

"Hattie is our first dog and we want to take really good care of her," Mr. Wong said, sounding slightly nervous. "We'll do all we can to make sure she's happy and has everything she needs."

I cleared my throat, seeing the perfect opportunity. "Actually, we might be able to help you with that," I said. "With our Dog Club."

Ms. Wong was nodding. "You mentioned that before," she said, sounding interested. "How does it work?"

We explained the club to the Wongs while Tim

gathered up the empty plates, Alice packed the cake away, and Caley played with the dogs.

"It sounds perfect," Ms. Wong said, looking at her husband, who nodded enthusiastically. "We'd like to sign Hattie up."

Kim, Sasha, and I squealed at that.

"As you can see, the girls adore Hattie," Alice said with a grin. "We all do. I think it will be good for her to spend some time here every week. And I know we'll love having her."

Sasha took Mr. Wong into Alice's office to fill out the forms to officially join the Dog Club while Kim and Ms. Wong headed over to Hattie. Hattie jumped up and gave Kim a big kiss on the cheek, then ran after the tennis ball Caley was throwing. I took out my camera and snapped a shot of Popsicle dropping a ball at Tim's feet, Boxer and Humphrey sniffing a chew toy, Caley snuggling Gracie, and Kim laughing as Hattie bounced at her feet.

A few minutes later Sasha came out of the office.

Mr. S and Popsicle ran over to her, and Kim and I followed.

"We have a new Dog Club client," I said happily.

"We really needed that," Kim said, sounding
relieved.

"And we get to keep seeing Hattie," Sasha added.
"I'd have missed her so much if she left for good."

I looked over at the fluffy little dog and nodded.
"Same."

"And this makes a space for a new dog to come to
the shelter," Kim said. "That's a good thing too."

It was true. Alice did her best to take in every dog
that needed a place to stay, but sometimes the shelter got
too full. Having a space open meant now a dog could
come here and make a home at the shelter, at least until
we found a family like the Wongs that wanted to adopt
a new dog.

The door to the shelter opened and Mrs. Washington came in. Gus raced to the door, excited to greet
his owner. I saw the Wongs watching as Gus leaped up

joyfully and licked her cheek.

Mrs. Washington laughed. "I missed you too," she said. "How was this guy today?" she asked us.

"Great like always," Sasha said, grabbing Gus's leash off the hook by the door and handing it to her.

"We'll post on the blog tonight," Kim said.

"And I took a couple of really cute pictures of him," I added. "They'll be up too."

Mrs. Washington smiled as she snapped Gus's leash onto his collar. "I always love reading about the fun he has here every day." She waved as the two of them headed out the door.

Now the Wongs stepped forward, and Ms. Wong smoothed back her hair nervously. "I think it's time for us to go too." She reached into her purse and pulled out a purple collar and leash.

I suddenly felt a lump in my throat. Hattie was really leaving!

"I can help you with those," Alice said calmly. She gently put the collar on Hattie and then petted her while Mr. Wong fumbled with the leash. Finally he had it secured.

"Okay then," he said, sounding uncertain.

Hattie looked at us, confused.

"You're going home," Kim said, and I could hear a hint of tears in her voice. "I bet they have a good dinner waiting for you."

"We got everything Alice suggested," Ms. Wong said. She bent down and petted Hattie. "Let's go home, girl."

We all watched as the Wongs led Hattie out. Hattie turned in the doorway, her brown eyes wide as she looked back at us.

"Good-bye, Hattie," we called.

And then she was gone.

"This is so sad," Sasha wailed.

Alice put an arm around her shoulder. "And happy too."

"I'm just glad she'll be coming to Dog Club," I said, sniffling a little. It was sad. But as Alice said, it was happy too.

"Definitely," Caley agreed.

"We should be sure to give the other dogs some extra attention," Kim said. She was stroking Boxer as she spoke. "They'll miss her and they don't understand what happened the way we do."

Of course Kim, the dog whisperer, thought of that! "Good point," I said, going over to Lily so I could give her a hug.

The shelter door opened again as other owners came to pick up their dogs. When the last one had gone, we helped Alice put away toys and then took one final look around.

"I know Hattie was just one dog, but it seems kind of empty in here without her," Caley said.

It did.

We headed home, the mix of happy and sad staying with me for the rest of the night.

8

"I can't believe we have another big essay for English," Kim said with a sigh as we sat down at our lunch table. "I feel like we just handed in the one about our volunteer work."

I knew Kim had struggled with that, though in the end she got an A. "This one sounds a little easier," I said, peeling the top off my yogurt. We were almost done with the Eleanor Roosevelt book, and this new essay was writing about someone you admired. "Who are you guys going to write about?"

"I'm going to write about my mom," Sasha said, mixing the dressing into her salad. "Sometimes she drives me crazy but she's pretty amazing, raising me on her own and running a law firm and everything."

"Yeah, you should call the essay 'Superwoman,'" I said.

Sasha grinned. "What about you guys?"

Just then Rachel stopped at our table, a concerned look on her face. "Hey," she said. "Have you guys seen this?" She held up a flyer and I immediately recognized the swirly letters of Pampered Puppy.

"Yeah, they're all over town," I said with a sigh.

"Actually, this is a new one," Rachel said, passing it over hesitantly. "They seem to be taking a slightly different approach."

That didn't sound good. I took the flyer and the three of us bent over it.

Pampered Puppy Doggy Day Care is the best dog care center in Roxbury Park! We have experienced professionals ready to shower your pet with love. Your dog will love our superior facilities and newly installed dog run. Best of all, we create an individual dog care program for each dog who comes through our doors. Sign up today for our special deal and treat your dog to the best care in town!

Below the text was a picture of two smiling professionals hugging a group of dogs—different caregivers, who hadn't been on the other flyers or in the video. Which meant the Pampered Puppy had a pretty big staff.

"Yikes," Sasha said. "This really is, um"—she searched for the word—"aggressive."

"Like an attack," I agreed. "On us." It was starting to seem like Brianna's mom was every bit as difficult as Brianna.

Kim held up a hand. "Not necessarily," she said. "I mean, they don't come out and say our club isn't as good as theirs."

"I guess not," I said, reading it over again. "But they

say that their dog care is the best in town, and the only other doggy day care is us."

"Yeah, but that could also just be a way to promote themselves, not to put us down," Sasha said. "You know, like how the deli next to the gas station is called the World's Best Deli."

"Maybe," I said slowly. "But either way, it's pretty attention grabbing."

"So is the promise of an individualized dog care plan," Sasha said, looking back at the flyer. "What is that anyway?"

None of us had an answer for that.

"We need to do something to get our club out there," I said finally. "To let people know we're great too."

"We'll help," Rachel called. She was sitting and eating with Emily, Dana, and Naomi but they were clearly keeping tabs on our conversation.

"That reminds me, I brought some flyers for you guys," Kim said, digging them out of her bag and passing them over.

Emily grabbed them. "We're on it," she said. "And if we happen to cover a few of the Pampered Puppy flyers, oh well."

I couldn't help grinning at that, though Kim looked concerned. "We don't want to damage their notices," she said.

"Don't worry, I'm just kidding," Emily said. "We'll play fair. Even though I'm not sure they will."

I worried she was right, but there was nothing we could do about that. There *was* something we could do to help our club though. "I say we print up a whole bunch of flyers and do what Pampered Puppy did and paper the town."

Sasha nodded. "Yeah, I was thinking that too. We haven't been very aggressive in our advertising, and now seems like a good time to start."

9

When I walked into the shelter with Coco and Gus, I nearly ran into Tim, who was dashing out.

"Sorry," he said, making sure Coco, Gus, and I were okay before he went on his way.

"Where's the fire?" I called.

"No fire," Tim said. "But I had the best idea and I need to get supplies."

With that, he was gone.

I shut the door behind me and began unclipping Coco and Gus from their leashes. "What's going on with Tim?" I asked Caley and Kim, who were already there.

"It's a mystery," Caley said. She was petting Oscar, who was curled up in his favorite spot on the windowsill.

"We were talking about playing dog tag and he suddenly raced out, shouting about his amazing idea," Kim said. She was on the floor cuddling Humphrey, Popsicle, Lily, and Gracie. Which would be impossible for most people, but somehow Kim was able to snuggle them all.

"Maybe he's figured out the cure for cancer," Caley said. She was playing fetch with Daisy, Boxer, and Coco, and Gus ran to join in.

"Or global warming," I said with a grin.

The door to the shelter opened and Sasha, Mr. S, and Hattie walked in. Hattie stood still for a moment, looking around the shelter in wonder. Lily caught sight of her and rushed over to say hi. Boxer, Popsicle, and Coco followed.

"I want to hug Hattie but I guess I have to wait my turn," I said, laughing as Hattie joyfully greeted her doggy friends. It was so good to see her back.

"She's the girl of the hour," Caley agreed.

We waited our turn, along with Kim, and finally got to snuggle the happy sheepdog. But only for a minute. Once she caught sight of her favorite red ball, she was off, Coco, Lily, and Gus right behind her as Sasha picked it up and tossed it across the room.

"Where's Tim?" Sasha asked.

We explained Tim's baffling exit.

"Oh, that sounds exciting," Sasha said. "I wonder what it is."

Then the front door opened and Tim came in, an old plastic laundry basket tucked under one arm.

"The greatest idea ever involves doing laundry?" Caley asked, one brow raised.

"Of course not," Tim said. "This isn't a laundry

basket; it's a basketball net."

Sasha frowned. "It's a bit big, isn't it?"

Tim laughed. "*Dog* basketball," he clarified.

Sasha, Kim, Caley, and I exchanged amused looks as Tim set the basket down in the center of the shelter. The dogs immediately came over to investigate but when they saw it wasn't food or a toy, they lost interest pretty fast.

"I'm not sure your target audience is convinced," Caley joked.

"That's because the game hasn't started yet," Tim said, rolling his eyes. He went into the food room, came out with a box of dog treats, and grabbed a blue rubber ball, which he threw across the room. Boxer, Lily, and Coco streaked after it, and Boxer came out the victor, ball in his mouth. But just as he was about to give it to Tim, Tim put the basket in front of his paws. "Drop it," he said firmly.

Boxer looked up, confused. Then he opened his mouth and the ball fell into the basket.

"Good dog!" Tim cheered exuberantly.

Boxer looked over at Lily, as though saying, "What's he talking about?" but then Tim rewarded him with a doggy treat and Boxer was in. The next time he got the ball, he dropped it into the basket and wagged his tail expectantly.

It didn't take the other dogs long to figure out the game, and soon all of them and all of us were playing dog basketball. I stopped after a few minutes to take some pictures but then jumped back into the action.

"This was a genius idea," I told Tim awhile later, wiping some sweat off my brow.

"That's just how I roll," Tim said smugly.

We all laughed but then Kim looked at the clock and turned serious. "We need to print out those flyers," she said, brushing some hair out of her face. "And I'm hoping Alice will be okay with us leaving a little early so we can get a bunch of them up tonight on our way home."

It had been so fun to run around with the dogs

that I'd almost forgotten the awful events of lunch. But Kim's words brought it all back.

"You guys are putting up more flyers?" Caley asked. She was panting a little; dog basketball was seriously strenuous.

"Yeah, to get the Roxbury Park Dog Club name out there," Sasha said.

"So people know there isn't just one doggy daycare in town," I added.

Tim was nodding. "That's a good idea," he said. "I can put some up too."

"Count me in," Caley said.

"Great," Kim said, smiling as she went into Alice's office to print out the flyers and ask about leaving early.

"Pampered Puppy really is making a splash," Caley said with a sigh. Humphrey had collapsed at her feet and she sat down next to him to give his belly a good rub.

"Yeah," Sasha said. We were all slowing down now and she was petting Boxer and Lily, who were sitting next to each other, tongues hanging out as they recovered from the game.

Kim came out of the office with the flyers. "Alice says it's fine if we leave in about fifteen minutes," she said, tucking the stack of papers into her backpack.

"Sounds good," I said, not fully meaning it. I'd much rather be playing with the dogs than sticking flyers up all over town. But of course we had to do it—nothing mattered more than making sure the club kept getting new members.

Hattie came over to me and dropped a Frisbee at my feet, then looked up, waiting.

"You still have energy?" I asked her, sending the Frisbee across the room. She ran after it, along with Coco, Gracie, and Daisy.

A few minutes later Ms. Wong came in and called Hattie. Hattie glanced over at her new owner, who gave a big smile. But then Hattie turned and followed her furry friends to get the Frisbee.

"She's having such a good time," I heard Caley tell

Ms. Wong as I threw the Frisbee for the dogs again. Lily and Boxer had joined in, so it was a bit of a mob scene. I took a quick photo when Hattie managed to wrestle the Frisbee from Boxer and came streaking back.

"Clever girl," I told her. "And now it's time for you to go home."

It took a little to convince Hattie that playtime with the Frisbee was over, but soon she was heading out with Ms. Wong, and Kim, Sasha, and I gathered up our stuff.

Kim passed some of the flyers over to Tim and Caley. "It's good we're doing this," she said. "I think it will help us get a few new members."

"I hope so," Caley said as we headed out.

It was chilly out, the sun low in the sky as we started up Main Street, posting flyers in every bit of empty space we saw. My fingers were freezing by the time we'd stapled up the last one and were walking down Spring Street.

"So now we wait," Kim said, "for the calls to start flooding in."

"I'll keep you posted," Sasha said, sounding hopeful.

I waved at my friends, then started toward my house, my fingers double crossed that maybe this would put the Pampered Puppy threat behind us for good.

The next day I was walking away from my locker when something cold, wet, and sticky sloshed against my back.

"Oh, I'm so sorry," an insincere voice said behind me. "I tripped."

I turned to see Brianna, an empty cup from Fresh and Fruity Smoothies in her hand.

"You got smoothie all over me," I said, hardly believing it even though it was trickling down my back.

"I'm so sorry," she said again, but the corners of her mouth were quivering as though she was about to burst into giggles.

I fled to the bathroom, which was empty, and took off my shirt. Luckily the smoothie was thick, so it hadn't spread over too much of the fabric. I rinsed my shirt off, accepting that I would smell like blueberries for the rest of the day, then put it back on. The wet spot in the back clung uncomfortably to my skin. I had a few minutes before homeroom would start so I stood in front of the hand dryer, trying to dry out or at least warm the spill. And to blink back the tears that were making my eyes blurry.

Brianna had done this on purpose, that I knew for sure. And I also knew that it was time to stop pretending that this was getting better because it wasn't; it was getting worse. Brianna was out to get me, and I had no idea what to do about it. Which meant only one thing.

It was time to get help.

I told Kim and Sasha everything at lunch.

"This is so not okay," Sasha said angrily as she inspected my shirt, which had dried but was crusty and stiff where the smoothie had landed.

"I don't understand why she's bothering you," Kim said, frowning. "You're, like, the nicest person ever."

"And you've never done anything to her," Sasha added, sending a glare in Brianna's direction. Brianna was on the other side of the cafeteria with a few girls from my math class, so she didn't notice, but Sasha's anger on my behalf was comforting. As was Kim's clear dismay.

"We have to make her stop," Sasha said determinedly.

Kim nodded. "Yeah, she needs to back off and leave you alone."

"But how do I make her do that?" I asked. Even in my yucky shirt I felt a million times better now that my friends knew what was going on. "My dad always told me to ignore bullies, but that totally hasn't worked."

Kim wrinkled her brows thoughtfully. "Remember in fourth grade when we had that workshop on how to handle teasing?" she asked Sasha.

Sash frowned. "Kind of."

"Well, the speaker had all this advice, like being more confident," Kim said. "Because apparently that makes it harder for kids to pick on you."

"Taylor's pretty confident though," Sasha said.

"Usually," I said. "But the stuff Brianna says does make me feel bad."

"That was another tip," Kim said. "That you aren't supposed to show when you get upset. Which is pretty tough to do when someone pours a smoothie all over you."

"Or tells you you're clumsy," Sasha said sympathetically, squeezing my hand. She knew that had come from Brianna without me even saying, which just showed what a great friend she was.

Kim was scowling. "You're not clumsy," she said. "You're tall and graceful like a supermodel. She's probably just jealous."

I snorted but Sasha was nodding. "That's what my mom says," she said. "That people who tease do it because of their own reasons, not because of you. Like they're jealous or feel insecure about something."

It was hard to imagine Brianna being insecure

about anything. And I was still thinking about what Kim had said. "You know, I think I probably do let it show when Brianna hurts my feelings," I said. I was sure she'd seen the tears in my eyes today when she gave me the smoothie-bath. "Do you think it would help if I shrugged more stuff off?"

"It's worth a try," Sasha said, taking a bite of her salad.

I'd been so focused on our conversation that I'd forgotten to eat but now I realized I was hungry. "Maybe there are other ways I can show her I don't care, like making a joke or laughing off what she says," I said, opening my yogurt and mixing it.

"That could work," Kim agreed. "And maybe you can also just walk away instead of responding."

"Or look blank, like what she's saying doesn't make any sense," Sasha said.

I nodded as I ate, feeling good about the Brianna situation for the first time, well, ever. My friends' ideas could really solve this once and for all.

"Oh, and you guys," I said, "guess what business her mom owns."

Kim drew in a sharp breath. "Not Pampered Puppy!"

I nodded. "Yeah, and Brianna keeps telling me that her mom is going to put us out of business."

"Well, then that's another thing she's wrong about," Sasha said firmly.

"Yeah, no one bullies any of us or our Dog Club," Kim agreed.

The bell rang just as I took my last bite of yogurt. "Thanks so much, you guys," I said, feeling super grateful to have such good friends on my side.

"That's what we're here for," Kim said.

And Sasha nodded. "Team Taylor forever!"

10

It was my night to clean up after dinner, so I was in the kitchen filling the sink with soapy water. My dad was out and Jasmine had made lasagna, which had been yummy but was a pain to clean since it involved a lot of dishes and scrubbing the baking pan, which was crusted with dried cheese and noodles. It was going to take me forever to get it all done. I was just piling the first round of pots in to soak when I heard the front door open.

"Hey, girls, I brought you something," my dad called as he came into the kitchen carrying a bakery box. "Cookies from Trattoria Romana," he said, opening the box with a flourish.

"Delish," Anna said, swooping in to grab the first one.

I couldn't help glaring at her, and she smiled at me sweetly. "How's the cleanup going?" she asked.

I rolled my eyes and grabbed a cookie. Trattoria Romana had the best Italian food in town and their cookies were awesome, all buttery and sweet. I picked one that was crescent shaped and sprinkled with powdered sugar.

"How was your client dinner, Dad?" Anna asked, reaching for a second cookie.

My dad looked confused for a second but then cleared his throat. "Productive," he said.

I was about to ask him more about it but he was busy fussing with the cookies. "I brought extras in case you want to take some to school tomorrow," he said as

Jasmine and Tasha came in.

"Thanks, Dad," I said. Kim and Sasha would be excited to share these. I'd have to make sure I brought enough for Emily, Rachel, Naomi, and Dana too.

"You can't take all of them, Taylor," Anna said, as though reading my mind.

"I'm sure Taylor isn't planning to steal all the cookies," my dad said mildly, loosening his tie.

"Last time you brought us brownies, Taylor took almost all of them," Anna reported.

"I brought them to share with my friends," I said crossly.

"Whatever," Anna said, rolling her eyes.

"Do you girls need me to help you divide up the cookies?" my dad asked.

I was instantly ashamed and I could tell Anna felt the same.

"No, Dad," we said, nearly in unison.

"Well, if you're sure you can handle things, I think I'll go upstairs and get out of my work clothes," my dad said.

He headed upstairs and Tasha gave us her social worker look. "You guys seem to have a lot of issues these days," she said, sitting on one of the stools at the island and selecting a green leaf-shaped cookie.

"The only issue I have is Anna bothering me all the time," I grumbled.

"If you stop being so annoying, I'll stop bothering you," Anna said, glaring at me.

"I'm not doing anything," I snapped. "You're the one picking a fight." Seriously, Anna was the only person I knew who could ruin something nice like my dad bringing us cookies.

"Just don't take them all," Anna said, heading out of the room.

"I get it," I hissed.

Jasmine and Tasha exchanged a look and headed upstairs, leaving me with my bad mood and a ton of dirty dishes.

It took me almost an hour but the kitchen was finally spotless, which I knew would make my dad happy.

I hoped he would understand that it was my way of thanking him for the cookies and apologizing for the fight with Anna. He probably would—my dad was smart like that.

I headed upstairs and was walking into my room when my phone vibrated with a text from Kim.

Check PP site. Will call u in 5.

Uh-oh.

I fired up my computer and logged onto the Pampered Puppy website. There was a new home page, written in bold print and dotted with cute drawings of dogs. None of which seemed that bad until I started reading it.

How do you know you can count on the people looking after your dog? We know you ask yourself this question anytime you trust pet sitters in a new setting. And if you are leaving your pet with young, inexperienced caretakers, you have good reason to worry. That's why Pampered Puppy offers something

new to Roxbury Park: trained professionals to care for
your pet. We guarantee safety and happiness—and
you'll know your dog is getting the best care possible
because you will get to see it in action anytime you
want with our live webcam! At Pampered Puppy
Doggy Day Care we offer you the peace of mind
that only comes with qualified professionals! And
that's the best deal out there!

My stomach was boiling as I read it a second time.
This was a clear attack on our Dog Club! I should have
guessed that Brianna's mom would be just like Brianna
and hit us where it hurt.

"This is just wrong," I said when Kim called a few
minutes later. I saw she'd set up a three-way line so
Sasha was on too. "Brianna's mom is totally going after
us."

"You were right," Sasha said, sounding really upset.
"They want to get their business going by ruining ours.
I didn't want to believe it, but it's obviously true."

"Yeah, it's pretty blatant," Kim said. I could hear the distress in her voice.

"How are we going to fight back?" I asked. My bedroom was usually my oasis, with my pictures all over the walls, my favorite books piled up on my bookcase, and my fluffy blue comforter. But tonight nothing was going to soothe me, and I began pacing.

"I think we should start a new campaign," Kim said. She'd clearly been thinking about this. "Pampered Puppy is saying we have no experience with dogs, but we do, and we need to let people know that."

"Oh, good idea," Sasha said. "How do we do it?"

"I'm thinking we make new flyers," Kim said. "And put on quotes from our dog owners saying how much they love our Dog Club. If people see how much our customers love us, they'll know we're fully capable of taking care of dogs."

"Smart," I said. "It's not just us saying we're good, but people who use the club speaking for us and saying we're awesome."

"It really is perfect," Sasha agreed. "And we can use the quotes we have on our website."

"That's what I was thinking," Kim said, clearly pleased we liked her plan.

"We should put pictures on too," Sasha said. "And we have tons of those from the blog."

"They don't look that good in black-and-white though," Kim said regretfully. The printer at the shelter was old and didn't do colors.

"I'll get my mom to make copies at her office," Sasha decided.

"That would be terrific," I said, thinking how cool it would be to have sleek, colorful ads for our Dog Club. "I just wish we could put in photos of us with the dogs."

"Me too," Kim said. "But my parents said no public pictures until I'm in high school." Which was exactly what my dad said.

"My mom too," Sasha said with a sigh. "Plus she's mad at me about the English quiz I failed, so now is not the time to ask her about that. I think she'll do the flyers though—she's a big supporter of the club."

My stomach dropped at her words—Sasha never failed things. But before I could ask her about it, she went on.

"And speaking of that quiz, I need to go so I can finish the reading for tomorrow," she said.

"Okay," Kim said. I could hear the concern in her voice but I knew she wanted to give Sasha the time she needed to get her homework done, just like I did. "We'll get on this tomorrow."

We ended the call. I needed to start my homework but first I clicked onto our website and copied down the best quotes so we could get started on our flyers at lunch the next day. It would be easiest if we could just use our cell phones to get the quotes, but since we couldn't turn them on in school, this was the next best thing. That way Sasha could give the flyer to her mom tomorrow night, and by the end of the week the whole town would know just how great the Roxbury Park Dog Club was!

11

"I brought cookies," I announced as I sat down at our lunch table. I'd grabbed the box on my way out, while Anna was upstairs getting her school stuff together, so there were plenty.

"Oh, too funny, so did I," Sasha exclaimed, holding up a Tupperware. "We'll have plenty of fuel while we design our flyers. Where are yours from?"

"My dad got them last night at Trattoria

Romana—he had a client dinner," I said, opening the top. A light scent of sugar and butter wafted out, fighting the bigger smells of overcooked vegetables and grease that always hung in a cloud over the cafeteria.

"Hey, that's what I brought too," Sasha said, sounding surprised. "My mom told me she ate there last night but she didn't mention that she was with your dad."

"My dad didn't say anything either," I said. Which was weird—my dad knew I loved that he worked with my best friend's mom. But there wasn't time to worry about that, not when we had flyers to design. "I copied some quotes down," I said, pulling out the paper from last night.

"Good," Kim said. She had taken three pieces of paper and spread them out on the table in front of her. "I was thinking we should start with three different designs, to keep it interesting."

"Great," Sasha said. "How should we do them?"

"I think a quote should go on the top," Kim said, beginning to write as she spoke. "Then a picture, then our information. It's straight to the point so people get the message fast."

"Sounds good," Sasha said, nodding. "And my mom is going to print them out tomorrow. I asked her at breakfast, and she's happy to help us."

"Awesome," I said, and Kim grinned.

"Taylor, do you want to email me pictures later?" Sasha asked. "I can set it all up on my mom's computer tonight."

"It's a plan," I said, scraping out the last of my yogurt, then grabbing a cookie. "Which pictures do you guys think we should use?"

"Definitely that one of Daisy, Gus, and Coco sleeping together," Sasha said immediately. She was done with her salad and had moved on to dessert too.

"That one is so cute," Kim agreed. "And I love that one of Popsicle and Mr. S both catching a Frisbee at the same time. We should use that one for sure." She popped the last bite of her sandwich into her mouth and grabbed a cookie.

Sasha nodded enthusiastically. "Yes, that's one of my favorites," she said.

I couldn't help feeling a flush of pride as they talked.

"There's also the one of Hattie and Humphrey where they're touching noses," Kim said. "And the one of Gus leaning on Boxer."

"It's hard to choose with so many great options," Sasha said.

"You guys are making me blush," I told them. They both stopped talking. "I didn't mean you should stop," I said, grinning. "Carry on!"

They laughed.

"Looks like the party's over here," Emily said, turning around to face our table.

"That's because we have cookies," I said, handing her my box. "Take some."

"Thanks," Emily said, reaching for it and passing it around their table.

"Take a lot," Sasha said. "We have doubles." She was eating a chocolate cream sandwich cookie that looked really good. I pulled her Tupperware over to see if there were any more like it.

"Check out our idea for our new flyers," Kim said, passing over the sketches.

"Wow, this quote is awesome," Rachel said. "'Our dogs love their time at the Roxbury Park Dog Club. It's a real find.'" That one was from the Cronins.

"You guys sure are popular," Naomi said, holding up another flyer. "'The staff at Roxbury Park are the most loving, responsible caregivers any dog owner could hope for,'" she read. That was Coco's owner.

"We're hoping the flyers will make us even more popular," Kim said, crunching on one of the pink leaf cookies.

"No doubt they will," Emily said, looking at the last flyer. "'Signing our dog up for the Roxbury Park Dog Club was the best choice we ever made!' That's a great endorsement."

"That one's my favorite," I agreed. It was from Mrs. Washington, and she'd said it to me on a day when

Gus was all covered with mud from playing dog tag. I'd been really worried she'd have a fit like Mrs. Whitman had with Clarabelle the poodle, but her reaction was the opposite.

"I think these are going to get you tons of business," Rachel said, passing back the nearly empty box of cookies.

I held up my hands. "I can't take it back till it's empty," I said. "Because if I eat one more cookie I'm going to explode!"

They laughed and took the remaining cookies as the bell rang. Sasha gathered up our designs for the flyers and we headed out, fortified with cookies and ready to fight for our Dog Club.

The last class of the day had ended and I was heading to my locker when I heard a familiar voice right behind me.

"Do you have asthma or something, New Girl?" Brianna asked, squeezing past two girls so she could walk next to me.

It sounded like a normal question, which was really surprising because we'd just left our math class and I'd seen her glaring at me when I got an answer right.

"No," I said. It was starting to occur to me that it was also a weird question.

"Oh, I assumed you did," she said. "Because you were making all those snorting noises in math."

Her words sucked the air out of my lungs. "What do you mean?" I asked. I hadn't been aware of how I was breathing, but maybe I was making noise without even realizing it? I had been pretty focused on the lesson because algebra was my favorite class.

"You didn't notice people looking at you?" Brianna asked, surprised. "It was pretty loud."

I shook my head, anxiety pricking at me. Of course it was possible she was making it all up to be mean, but what if she wasn't? Anna sometimes called me a mouth breather. Maybe when I wasn't thinking about it I breathed really loudly and made weird noises.

"Well, I'd be more aware in the future," Brianna

said, moving ahead of me but looking back for one last barb. "Oh, and let me know if you want any flyers from Pampered Puppy—you know, to give your clients when you guys go out of business once and for all."

I knew Brianna could see how much her words upset me, but at this point I didn't even care. The remark about flyers was a low blow, and what if I did really sound like a pig in my classes? I did a quick U-turn, nearly bumping into two boys from math, and practically ran through the crowd to Kim's locker.

"Do I breathe too loudly?" I asked her.

Kim was putting books into her backpack but she stopped immediately and looked at me, slightly confused but instantly reassuring. "No, you most certainly do not," she said.

"You're sure?" I asked. "You'd be honest? Because if I'm making snorting noises like a pig and other people notice, that's totally humiliating. And as my best friend, you're obligated to keep me from being totally humiliated."

Kim rested a hand gently on my arm. "I promise I will always let you know if I think you are in danger of total humiliation," she said. "And I would have told you ages ago if you sounded like a pig."

I was starting to calm down. Kim would tell me the truth, I knew that. And as I let it sink in, another truth hit me: Brianna had gotten me again. And not only did I forget every piece of advice I'd gotten from Kim and Sasha, but I'd totally fallen into her trap.

I sighed and leaned against Kim's locker. "It turns out I'm not so good at pretending stuff doesn't bother me," I said to Kim.

She patted my shoulder protectively. "Well, anyone would be upset if they thought they were snorting in class," she said, which made me laugh.

But as I walked back to my locker for my stuff, I couldn't help worrying that I'd never be able to stop Brianna from giving me a hard time.

And that was anything but funny.

12

"I think we have the whole town covered," Kim said, sounding satisfied as she taped up the last flyer from our stack. We'd raced into town right after school to put them up.

"I love how they stand out," Sasha said, looking at the town hall bulletin board, where we'd hung a flyer front and center.

"Your mom did a super job with them," I said. She'd used a glossy paper that made the flyers look like movie posters.

"It was a good design," Sasha said.

"With terrific photos," Kim added.

"I guess we're just a great team," I said. Then I checked my watch. "And we're a team that needs to get going because we have dogs waiting."

Now that downtown Roxbury Park was covered with our flyers, it was time to pick up dogs for Dog Club.

"See you guys in a few minutes," I called as I headed over to get Humphrey and Popsicle. Their home was only a block away, so in no time I had them leashed up and on the way to the shelter.

When I walked in I saw that Tim had a game of dog basketball going. Popsicle took one look and ran over to join Boxer, Lily, Gus, and Hattie, who had arrived before us with Kim. A moment later Sasha walked in with Mr. S and Coco.

"The gang's all here," Caley announced happily. "Which means it's time for dog tag."

She led the way outside, the dogs rushing to follow and the rest of us close behind. It was a gray day but warm and kind of humid.

"Taylor, you're it," Caley called, throwing me the ball. I tossed it across the yard. The dogs streaked after it while the humans ran. Hattie got it first, scooping it up and racing away as the bigger dogs arrived. They chased her over to Kim, and Kim was it. She threw the ball toward the far corner of the yard, and everyone began running again.

Not surprisingly, Humphrey was the first to take a break. He found a cozy spot under the big oak tree and settled down with a sigh. I sat down next to him, breathing hard from all the running, and stroked his silky ears. A few minutes later Hattie came over for a hug.

"Who's a sweet girl?" I asked her, snuggling her close. "Oh, and you have a new collar." It was green, which looked great with her shaggy white fur. She had a bright silver name tag that said "Hattie Wong" and listed the Wongs' phone number. "I bet you love your new home," I told her.

"I think she does," Kim agreed, dropping down next to me and scratching Hattie's ears. "She seems so happy since the Wongs adopted her."

She really did.

A moment later the ball zipped past and Hattie was up and after it.

"Break's over," Tim called, and Kim and I stood up to rejoin the game.

All too soon the owners were arriving. First was Mrs. Washington, with Mr. Wong on her heels. Gus raced up to greet his owner, but Hattie was playing in the corner with Popsicle and didn't look up when Mr. Wong called her.

"Maybe she didn't hear you," I said.

"Hattie," he called again, a bit louder this time.

Hattie looked over and then went back to her game. Which was typical of a puppy. Hattie hadn't had any real training and probably thought it was fine for her owner to wait until she was done playing.

Mr. Wong was frowning. "It seems like she doesn't

want to leave," he said.

I laughed. "She has so much fun when she comes here," I said. "Don't worry, we'll help."

Kim went over and stopped the game, then led Hattie over to Mr. Wong. Hattie jumped up to give Mr. Wong a kiss, then ran to say good-bye to her friends.

"I don't think she wants to come home," Mr. Wong said. It looked like he was trying to smile but it wasn't quite working. He was probably in a rush.

"I'll get her," I said, taking her leash from his hands and heading over to Hattie. She stood quietly while I snapped it on and then allowed me to lead her to her owner.

"Thanks for the help," Mr. Wong said. The corners of his mouth were turned down. "I guess I needed it."

"She just loves being with her friends," Kim said. "But if you're firm she'll learn to leave when you say, not when she decides she's ready."

Her words were warm and reassuring, but Mr. Wong still looked upset as he carefully walked Hattie out.

"It's hard to be a first-time dog owner," Alice said as the door closed behind them.

I hadn't realized she had come out of her office to say good-bye to the dogs.

"There's so much to learn," she went on, bending down to pet Gracie, who had her chewed-up teddy in her mouth.

"The Wongs are lucky to have a dog as sweet as Hattie," I said. Oscar was twining around my ankles and I knelt to stroke his soft fur.

"And Hattie's lucky to have them," Kim added. "They're so nice."

Alice nodded. "They clearly care about her a great deal, and that's what matters most."

When the last of the owners had picked up their dogs, Kim, Sasha, and I said good-bye and headed out.

"I'm so glad we got our flyers up," Sasha said as we headed for home.

"Has anyone called or emailed yet?" Kim asked her.

Sasha shook her head. "Alice hasn't forwarded anything to me."

Kim's face fell.

"Give it time," I told her. "The flyers have only been up for a few hours. I bet at least one potential client will get in touch tonight."

"And I'll text you guys the minute they do," Sasha promised.

We said good-bye and I headed home for my night to cook dinner. I kept an eye on my phone for the rest of the night, but it never rang.

It was misty the next morning as Kim and I stood on the corner of Spring Street waiting for Sasha. The air was heavy, which meant rain was coming, and I hoped we'd make it to school before it began.

"I bet she's on her way," I said, taking out my phone in case she'd sent a text I didn't hear. But there were no missed messages.

"She said she was going to be up late with her homework last night," Kim said worriedly. "I hope she didn't oversleep."

But just then we saw her running up the block in big blue rain boots that would trip anyone but graceful Sasha.

"Is everything okay?" I asked as she came up. Then I saw the expression on her face and my heart dropped. "What's wrong?"

"Have you guys seen the latest on the Pampered Puppy website?" she asked in a tight voice.

Kim and I both shook our heads.

Sasha was pulling out her phone. "It turns out we need to start keeping tabs on these people because they just keep getting worse," she said. "Look at this."

Kim and I bent our heads over the small screen. The mean ad that had been there before was replaced by quotes from their clients.

"They copied us!" I exclaimed indignantly. Brianna's mom clearly didn't believe in playing fair.

"Yeah, but it's even worse than that," Sasha said. "Look at the first quote."

Kim took the phone and read the text out loud.

"'I've tried other places in town, but only Pampered Puppy takes the right kind of care of my dog. They treat her like she should be treated.'"

"That's not *that* bad," I started to say, wanting to keep things positive.

But then Kim looked up, and I could tell she was fighting back tears. "It's written by Mrs. Whitman, Clarabelle's owner."

Her words were like a slap. Mrs. Whitman had been so angry when we allowed fluffy white Clarabelle to get muddy the day after she'd been groomed. And now Pampered Puppy had her telling everyone what a bad job she thought we'd done.

I opened my mouth to say something positive, but nothing came to me.

Because this was really bad.

13

It had been a hard morning, and I was so ready to get to lunch to commiserate with Sasha and Kim that I skipped stopping at my locker and headed right to the cafeteria when the bell rang. But it turned out that was a terrible idea: the moment I stepped into the steamy buffet area, the first person I saw was Brianna. She smiled when she noticed me and headed over. Uh-oh.

I braced myself, ready to keep my expression casual

no matter what she said.

"You must have been so embarrassed in science, New Girl," Brianna began.

I felt a warmth creep across my face as I remember the humiliating moment she was bringing up. Ms. Lewis had called on me to answer a really simple question about photosynthesis, but I'd been distracted, thinking about Pampered Puppy, and said the totally wrong thing. People had snickered, and I saw one girl rolling her eyes. It just figured that Brianna would bring it up.

She was eyeing me now, waiting to see my reaction. I decided to try laughing it off and opened my mouth, letting out a giggle. It was too high and too loud. Brianna stepped back and a crease appeared between her brows, like she thought I might be going insane. "I can see it really bothered you," she said. "I don't blame you. It was totally humiliating when everyone laughed."

"Not everyone," I said quickly, because they hadn't. Some people hadn't been paying attention and didn't even notice. But then I remembered I was supposed to act like I didn't care, so I shrugged.

Brianna didn't seem to notice the shrug. "Right, I can see how you'd want to believe that," she said silkily. "Honestly, you should have seen your face. I wish I'd had a camera."

With that she flounced off to go ruin someone else's day. Or more likely plot how to next ruin mine. I sighed. Showing I didn't care wasn't working so well, probably because I did care, a lot. And I wasn't so good at hiding it.

The room was starting to fill up, so I headed over to get my yogurt. I wasn't hungry but I figured I'd be even more out of it if I didn't eat something. And I didn't want to risk another mortifying experience like the one in science. I was in line to pay when Kim and Sasha arrived.

"Hey," Sasha said, grinning when she saw me.

Kim smiled too and that helped a lot. No matter how bad things got with Brianna or Pampered Puppy, I always had Kim and Sasha, and that was everything.

We headed over to our table, greeted our friends, and then got down to business.

"I was thinking about it," Kim said, unwrapping her sandwich. "And the thing with Clarabelle wasn't something we did wrong, not really. I mean, dogs play outside and sometimes they get dirty. We were taking good care of her and she was safe. That's what matters, not a little mud."

Sasha was nodding. "That's a good point," she said. "And Mrs. Whitman hadn't asked us to keep Clarabelle clean."

"Or to keep her inside," I added. I was feeling a little better as I opened my yogurt.

"Right," Kim said, nodding. "I mean, we should have been more clear about what we do in the club, but we didn't do anything wrong. We really did take good care of Clarabelle, and she had a lot of fun at our Dog Club."

I was nodding but Sasha was starting to frown. "How do we tell people that, though?" she asked. "I agree we weren't at fault, but can we post that on our website?"

I shook my head. "Definitely not." I didn't know much about running a business but I knew we couldn't get into some kind of battle of words with Mrs. Whitman. We'd sound like we were accusing her, and nothing good would come of that.

"The point is that we have an answer if any potential customers ask us about Mrs. Whitman's quote," Kim said. She set down her sandwich and leaned forward. "I think people looking for a doggy day care will check us out and also look into Pampered Puppy. Our job is to present our club in the best way we can, which our flyers totally do. And to be able to answer any questions honestly and openly, which we can."

Now Sasha was nodding. "And if someone asks us what Mrs. Whitman is talking about, we can say it was a case of a dog having so much fun she got a little dirty."

"Exactly," Kim agreed.

As they began eating again, I licked some yogurt off

my spoon. Everything Kim and Sasha said made sense, yet one thing nagged at me: What if people just listened to Mrs. Whitman and never even called to hear our side of things?

But there was no point in worrying about that. We'd have to hope that people would give us the benefit of the doubt.

Or better yet, see our flyers and know right off that we were the best ones to take care of their dogs!

"I have a business dinner tonight, girls," my dad said at breakfast the next morning. "Are you okay fending for yourselves?"

"No problem," Tasha said. "We've got it covered."

"Is it another client dinner?" I asked. I was eating the granola Jasmine had made over the weekend, and it was really good. Except she always put in dried apricots, and I didn't like those.

My dad hesitated for a moment, then nodded.

"With Sasha's mom?" I asked.

My dad looked surprised. "Why do you ask?"

That was kind of weird. They worked together, so my question seemed normal, at least to me. "I just like hearing about it," I said, picking out a soggy slice of dried apricot and setting it next to my bowl.

My dad smiled. "Right," he said. "I think she will be there, yes."

"You should make plans for something fun," I said, remembering how great it was when our families were at Lake George together for a whole month over the summer. "Like maybe a weekend trip or a picnic." Kim could come along too.

"Those are nice ideas," my dad said. "But this is really more of a business event." He picked up his empty bowl and rinsed it out. He usually had to leave a few minutes before we did.

"Dad did say it was a client dinner," Anna pointed out as my dad blew us a kiss and headed for the door.

I ignored her and pulled another apricot from my cereal.

"Can you stop being disgusting with your food?" Anna asked, annoyed.

Now I glared. "I'm not doing anything," I snapped.

"You have that gross little pile of apricots," Anna said, gesturing with her spoon. "It's totally killing my appetite."

I was about to say something biting when Tasha nodded. "She's right, it's nasty," she agreed.

Now I glared at her. What a backstabber.

Tasha held up her hands. "I'm just saying, maybe cover them with a napkin or something."

I practically threw my napkin over them.

"Or you could just eat them," Jasmine added. "They're good for you."

"Yeah, I don't know what kind of person doesn't like apricots," Anna said. She was clearly thrilled everyone agreed with her.

I picked up my stuff and stalked over to the sink. Now it was my appetite that was gone.

Being the youngest sister was definitely the worst.

14

"We are the champions!" Tim shouted, holding his arms up in victory, then reaching over to give me a high five.

I slapped his hand with gusto, then bent down to snuggle Gracie. "You were the star with that last-minute basket," I told her, kissing the top of her soft head.

We'd spent the afternoon at the shelter in a high-energy and often hilarious game of doggy basketball. Tim and I coached Gracie, Popsicle, Daisy, and Lily, while Kim and Caley led Boxer, Mr. S, Gus, and Coco. Sasha had been the ref, and Humphrey opted for a sideline role.

"I think you guys had a flagrant foul by Lily," Caley said with a pretend pout, "the way she grabbed the basket in her mouth and tipped it over so Boxer missed his shot. I'm calling for a rematch."

"That was great strategy," Tim said, running his fingers through his black hair and making it stand on end. "But Taylor and I will take you guys on any day."

"That's right," I said, grinning. "And be careful you don't question the integrity of the ref."

Sasha grinned. "Actually, I missed that because I was trying to get Humphrey to cheerlead."

We all laughed at that. It had been another terrific day at Dog Club. Well, except for one thing: Hattie hadn't come. The Wongs had left a message about not picking her up but they didn't say why. We were all a little worried, plus we missed her. The shelter wasn't the same without our Hattie.

The front door opened and Mr. Washington came in. Gus was busy playing tug-of-war with Boxer, and Mr. Washington looked pleased as he watched. After a minute or two, Gus had lost and he went over to his owner, panting slightly from his active day.

"Looks like he got a good workout today," Mr. Washington said as he stroked Gus's head.

"We all did," Caley said with a grin.

Mr. Washington smiled as he set out with Gus, passing Mrs. Cronin on his way. Popsicle rushed up to greet her owner while Humphrey took his time walking over.

"How were my babies today?" Mrs. Cronin asked. She was in a silky suit and heels from her job at the bank but still got right down to hug her dogs.

"Magnificent as always," I told her.

"That's what I like to hear," she said as Popsicle planted a big wet kiss on her cheek.

We waved as they headed out. A moment later, Daisy's and Coco's owners arrived, and then all the Dog

Club dogs were gone, except of course for Mr. S.

"Can you guys just pick up the toys and laundry basket before you leave?" Alice asked. She had come out of her office to say good-bye to the dogs, and her Snoopy shirt was covered with fur. I looked down and saw that my red T-shirt was the same. I guess there must have been extra shedding during the game of doggy basketball. "And then I think we're all set."

"Sure," Sasha said. She'd been snuggling with Lily and Mr. S but stood up to start gathering toys.

Just then the front door opened again and Ms. Wong walked in. I automatically looked behind her to see if she'd brought Hattie, but it was just Ms. Wong, brushing back her hair and looking nervous.

My stomach clenched up.

"Is everything okay?" Alice asked. Her voice was calm but her face was tense and I knew she was worried too. Why would Ms. Wong come here alone, after Dog Club? Was something wrong with Hattie?

"Everything is fine and Hattie is well," Ms. Wong

138

said, sounding hesitant. "It's just . . . we've made a change, and I felt I owed it to you to tell you in person."

Sasha glanced at me, her brow furrowed, and Kim was biting her lip. We all moved closer to Ms. Wong, waiting. Even the dogs seemed to pick up on the tension in the room and played quietly.

"You've been wonderful allowing us to adopt Hattie," Ms. Wong said. "And I know she has a good time when she comes to visit. But after thinking about it, we've decided to take Hattie out of the Dog Club."

There was a moment of stunned silence, and then Ms. Wong went on.

"Hattie's having trouble following commands, so we want her to go to a program that supports what she's learning in her weekend obedience classes," she said, twisting a lock of her long black hair. "And my husband and I are also worried that it confuses Hattie to keep coming to the shelter. She might think we plan to leave her here and not understand that she lives with us now."

Kim shot me a stricken look. I grabbed her hand on

one side and Sasha's on the other. This was awful and we had to talk Ms. Wong out of it!

Alice started to speak, but Ms. Wong held up a hand. "I know how much you love her, and we appreciate that, we really do," she said. "But Hattie is going to go to the nicer dog day care, the one at Pampered Puppy. They're going to develop a program to help with her training. It's the right thing for Hattie, and I hope you understand."

Kim was squeezing my hand so hard it hurt, and Sasha's eyes were wide with dismay. I felt like I'd been hit in the stomach. Hattie was going to Pampered Puppy? We couldn't let this happen.

I drew in a breath to protest, to beg Ms. Wong to reconsider, but then Alice glanced at all of us and I knew she was the one who needed to speak.

"We know you want what's best for Hattie," Alice said carefully. "Please know she's always welcome here."

"Thank you for understanding," Ms. Wong said. She walked out, her heels clicking on the wooden floor as she went, closing the door firmly behind her.

"Alice, how can we let her take Hattie away?" Kim cried.

"We have to try to talk her out of it," Sasha said. There were tears in her eyes, and Mr. S, sensing her distress, rushed over and pressed himself against her legs. She scooped him up and cuddled him close. "We can help train Hattie without some stupid specialized program. And we love Hattie way more than the professionals at Pampered Puppy."

"I know how sad this makes all of you," Alice said with a sigh. "But the Wongs are first-time owners trying to find their way, and it's not our place to tell them how to do it, not if they don't ask for our help. And I think they've sent a pretty clear message that what they need right now is some space."

"Do you really think being here was confusing for Hattie?" I asked. I was leaning against the wall patting Boxer. He clearly sensed the mood of the room and was being unusually calm.

"I don't think so," Alice said, pulling a piece of dog fur off her shirt. "Dogs are smart and Hattie knows the Wongs are her people."

"Mr. S knew right away that he lived with me," Sasha agreed. She still sounded slightly tearful, though I could tell it helped that Mr. S was snuggled in under her chin, warm and cozy. "He wasn't confused at all."

"If the Wongs really thought Hattie didn't understand, why didn't they talk to us?" Kim asked. She had slid down to sit on the floor, and Lily and Gracie were in her lap. "They always acted like everything was fine."

"Actually, now that I think about it, Ms. Wong did seem a little worried sometimes at pickup," Caley said with a sigh. "I didn't think it was a big deal or I would have said something. But looking back now, I can see it." She was starting to gather toys, and I went to help her.

"But what exactly made her worried?" Kim asked.

"I think it was the way Hattie didn't go right over to her," Caley said.

"But some dogs don't greet their owners first thing," I said, thinking of how Gus had finished his game with Boxer before greeting Mr. Washington today.

"Right, but remember the Wongs don't have as much dog experience as you," Alice reminded us. "To them it might have seemed like Hattie was having more fun here than she does at home with them."

"But I'm sure that's not true," Sasha burst out. "Hattie loves them; you can see it so clearly if you just look."

"I guess they weren't looking at the right things," I said sadly.

"But Pampered Puppy," Sasha moaned. "How can they send her there instead of to us, where she belongs?"

None of us had an answer to that because it was just too awful. Not only had we lost Hattie but we'd lost a customer, something the Dog Club simply could not afford.

We finished the cleanup and headed for home.

"Maybe Hattie will come back to visit," Sasha said when we got to the corner where we separated.

"Yeah, maybe," I said, trying to sound upbeat.

But I think we all knew that our time with Hattie had come to an end and there was nothing we could do to change it.

We were at lunch the next day, picking at our food, when Brianna sailed up to our table, a smile on her face. My whole body stiffened as I waited for whatever nasty thing she was about to say.

"My mother told me we have a new client," she said cheerfully. "A family whose dog used to go to your day care but thought you didn't do a good job."

"We know," Sasha said shortly. "Hattie. And they weren't upset with us, they were just . . . whatever; it's complicated."

Brianna's forehead wrinkled. "No, it's not Hattie," she said. "It's another dog."

There was no pretending that we didn't care about this. The three of us were stricken.

"Who is it?" Kim asked in a tight voice.

Now Brianna was smiling again, knowing she'd gotten to us. "Circa maybe? I forget the dog's exact name," she said cheerfully. "We have so many after all." With that she headed off, leaving the three of us in a panic.

"She has to be lying," Kim said. "The Cronins and Washingtons would never leave us."

"The Simmonses either," I added, thinking of how Coco's family were always so enthusiastic about the club. But my chest was tight. Clearly Brianna knew something, and that something was not good.

"Maybe she meant Clarabelle?" Kim asked.

Sasha was fumbling in her bag and a moment later she pulled out her phone.

"If an aide sees that, you'll lose your phone," Kim said urgently.

"This is an emergency," Sasha said, quietly turning it on. "You guys keep a lookout while I go to their website and see who the dog is."

Kim and I kept our eyes glued on the lunch aides,

who were busy breaking up a food fight at the other end of the cafeteria. After a moment Sasha sucked in a sharp breath.

"Who is it?" I asked, almost not wanting to know.

Sasha stuffed her phone into her bag, her hands shaking. "It's Sierra," she said in a choked voice.

Kim and I looked at each other, eyes wide. Sierra had been the one dog we hadn't been able to handle, the one dog we'd asked to leave the Dog Club. And now she was at Pampered Puppy. This was even worse than I'd feared.

Sasha went on. "The Finnegans have this quote about how they thought their dog was a lost cause, that no one could handle her, but the professionals"—her voice trembled as she said the word—"at Pampered Puppy totally saved her. She's obedient and well behaved and they are over the moon about it. That's what they said: 'over the moon.'"

We let this dreadful news sink in.

"Do they say anything about how we couldn't manage Sierra?" Kim finally asked in a small voice.

Sasha shook her head. "No, but people will figure it out."

Kim nodded. "Yeah, I know."

The bell rang but none of us moved.

"Everything okay over here?" Rachel asked as she and her friends stood up.

Kim gave her a watery smile. "Just a little problem with the Dog Club."

"Let us know if we can do anything," Dana said, patting Kim's shoulder as she passed.

"You guys will fix it," Emily said confidently. "You always do."

The three of us looked at each other and I knew what Sasha and Kim were thinking: Emily was right, we *had* always figured out how to handle the problems that had faced our club before. But we'd never faced a problem as big as this one.

And it was starting to look like this time there was nothing we could do to fix it.

15

A few days later I was heading to my locker after the final bell when I saw Brianna heading toward me. Without even thinking about it I ducked into the nearest empty classroom to wait while she passed. It was quiet and I leaned against the wall, closing my eyes.

"Is there something I can help you with?"

My eyes flew open. A teacher I didn't know had come in and was staring at me with a puzzled look.

"Um, no; thanks anyway," I mumbled, hustling out.

I glanced down the crowded hall and saw that Brianna had passed. And that was when it hit me how bad things were: I was actually hiding from a girl at my school, creeping around like a criminal to avoid running into her. It was absurd, but like the problem with the Dog Club, I had no idea how to fix it.

I walked slowly to my locker and grabbed my stuff, then headed out to meet Kim and Sasha. It was our new habit to meet outside the school so that whoever got there first could turn on her phone and check the Pampered Puppy website to see what new and awful information it held.

Today the first person was Kim. She was standing under an oak tree, phone in hand and a frown on her face.

"More bad news?" I asked as I walked up.

"The same, I guess," Kim said. "Lots of people saying how much they love Pampered Puppy. They must have almost twenty clients, with more people signing up every day."

"And no new clients for us," I said. "Unless Alice

sent Sasha a call during the day today."

"She didn't," Sasha said, coming up behind us, slightly breathless. "I just checked."

"Too bad," I said, hoisting my bag over my shoulder.

The three of us started down the path together.

"It's been a day of bad news," Sasha said gloomily. "I failed my math test and Ms. Rodriguez is calling my mom to talk about it. She says she's worried about my missed homework and now this."

I stopped in my tracks. "Sash, what is going on?" I asked.

Kim looked equally troubled as Sasha's eyes filled with tears. "I just don't have time to get everything done," Sasha wailed. "I'm up until midnight every night but then I'm so tired I can't actually study."

"Can we help?" Kim asked.

Sasha shook her head and we started walking again. "I need to figure out how to manage everything better," she said, sniffling a little. "And I know I will.

Eventually anyway." She sighed. "My mom is going to be so mad when she gets that call."

I squeezed her arm sympathetically.

"Let's not talk about that anymore," Sasha said as we crossed the street. The sun was shining and the air smelled like crisp leaves and mowed grass. "What's the latest on the Pampered Puppy website?"

Kim and I told her about all the new clients the Pampered Puppy had.

Sasha pulled out her phone. "I don't believe it," she said. "I bet they're making some of these people up."

That made me laugh. "So Mrs. Flynn who says her dog has never been so happy isn't real?"

"Exactly," Sasha said firmly, almost tripping over a bump on the sidewalk because she was looking up the Pampered Puppy website on her phone.

"It would be funny if they were all totally pretend and—" I began, but then Sasha gasped.

"What?" I asked, my skin prickling.

"Listen to this," she said angrily. "It's their latest ad.

'Why bother with second-rate care when you can get first-rate professionals to watch over your dog? Come to Pampered Puppy Doggy Day Care, the best doggy daycare in town!'"

"I can't believe this," I said, gritting my teeth. "They are totally putting us down."

"And getting more clients because of it," Kim said, twisting a lock of hair.

"And of course they have that quote from the Finnegans right under it," Sasha said bitterly.

"I wish the Finnegans were made-up," I muttered darkly. The more I thought about all of it, the angrier I got. "You guys, we can't let Pampered Puppy get away with this. We have to retaliate."

"We can try to put more content on our website, like they do," Kim said, looking at me uncertainly. "And update it every day if we can find the time. Is that what you mean?"

"Yes, but more too," I said. "They keep insulting us, so maybe it's our turn to say something nasty about them." As soon as I said the words I felt funny, like I'd swallowed an apple whole. Sasha and Kim looked uneasy too.

"I'm not sure," Kim began. "I mean, I see what you're saying, but it doesn't feel like us, you know?"

"That's true," Sasha said. "But my mom does always say that when it comes to business you need to fight fire with fire." She didn't sound fully convinced though.

We'd reached the corner of Montgomery and Elm, where Sasha was turning to go to dance, Kim was going straight to get to the Rox, and I was turning left to go home and start dinner.

"Let's think about it," I said. "Because it might not be the way our club does business. But if it's a choice between that and losing our club . . ." It hurt just to say those words.

"We'll think about it," Kim agreed. The corners of her mouth turned down.

We waved and went our separate ways. My whole body felt heavy as I walked. I wished we were heading to the shelter together. Right now I needed some dog time to lift my spirits, which were about as low as they could get.

But instead all that awaited me was an empty house, homework, and a meal to prepare. Oh, and a sister to tease me about it.

This was really turning into a bad day.

And it got worse. I'd gotten distracted looking at examples of advertising, trying to think of a way to drum up business for the club, and the hamburgers I'd been cooking all burned. Anna complained the whole meal, and no one ate very much.

I offered to help Tash wash up since burned pans were such a drag to clean, but she waved me upstairs. An hour later guilt was still gnawing at me, along with something else: hunger. Even I hadn't eaten much of my awful dinner. So I headed down to the kitchen for a snack.

When I walked in I heard someone rustling in the

pantry. I hoped it was Tash or Jasmine, or even my dad, but it was Anna, who came out holding a box of crackers. She scowled when she saw me. "That meal was the worst," she told me.

"I know," I said through clenched teeth. "I already said I was sorry like a hundred times."

Anna was getting some cheese out of the fridge to go with her crackers. I opened a cabinet and pulled out a box of chocolate chip cookies. I was hoping we were done talking, but when Anna saw the cookies she spoke right up.

"Don't eat all of them," she said, pointing to the box with a piece of string cheese.

"I won't," I grumbled.

"You always say that but then you just go ahead and do whatever you want," Anna said, making a cheese-and-cracker sandwich. "Like with the cookies Dad brought home from Trattoria Romana. Or when you cut up *Your Roxbury Park*."

She never forgot anything! "I said I won't eat them

all," I huffed. "Do you want me to write out a contract or something?"

Anna shook her head. "You can joke, but seriously, Taylor, try to think about someone other than yourself for once."

I opened my mouth to respond but suddenly it was all too much: Pampered Puppy, the Finnegans, the new ad, and Brianna, the person who had me cowering in my own school. A fight with Anna was more than I could bear. So instead of answering, I burst into tears. Which shocked me, but not as much as it shocked Anna.

Her mouth actually fell open as I sobbed. "Taylor, it's okay," she said, reaching out a hand to touch my arm.

But I jerked away, embarrassed to be falling apart like this but also angry. Really angry. "You're so mean to me all the time!" I shouted through my tears, my voice snuffly. "Why do you hate me so much?"

Anna sat down on a stool and rubbed her face for a moment. When she looked up, there were tears in her eyes. "You're my sister, Taylor. I don't hate you." Her voice wobbled a little.

"You sure act like you do," I said. My tears were finally slowing down, and I grabbed a napkin to wipe my face.

"Sometimes I get angry but I could never hate you, I promise," she said.

I shoved the cookies back into the cabinet. I wasn't hungry anymore and I didn't want to talk to Anna. I just wanted to go upstairs and hide in my room, possibly forever.

But when I started for the door, Anna stopped me. "Taylor, you're right; sometimes I am mean," she said quietly. "And I owe you an apology for that."

Now I was the one who was shocked. Anna never admitted to doing something wrong, not ever.

"Why do you do it?" I asked, now more curious than anything else.

Anna let out a long sigh, then smiled at me slightly. "I'll tell you if you eat some cookies," she said. "I don't want you starving in your own house because of something I said."

I could live with that deal. I took the cookies out again and sat on the stool next to Anna.

She stared at her hands for a moment, then took a deep breath. "Honestly, I guess I'm jealous of you," she said.

I almost choked. "Jealous of me? Why?" I asked. Anna was smart and pretty and popular—she had everything. What could she possibly think I had that she didn't?

"You're the baby of the family," she said. "The cute one. The girl everyone fusses over and takes care of, the one who gets all the attention."

"Really?" I asked, floored. I never felt like I got all the attention. In fact, it often seemed like my sisters were always talking about things I was too young to understand. I was constantly trying to worm my way into their conversation, to get them to talk about something I was interested in too. Oh. Maybe that was what

Anna meant. Because I did do a good job of getting Tash and Jasmine to talk about what I wanted to talk about once I put my mind to it. It had never occurred to me how that might affect Anna.

"Jasmine and Tasha drop everything when you come in," Anna said, a bitter edge to her voice. "Like tonight they were so nice about you burning dinner. If it was me, they'd have made me cook something new."

That was probably true. "But isn't that because you're older? It seems to me like the three of you are a team and I'm the one tagging along, always behind."

Anna shook her head. "Tash and Jasmine are the team, and you're their mascot," she said. "The one left out is me."

"They love you though," I said. I knew that for sure. But the rest of it was kind of hard to wrap my mind around. I'd never thought about Anna as being the fourth wheel. But hearing her talk, it was starting to sound like maybe I'd been missing something. "Why didn't you ever say anything about this before?"

"Like what?" Anna asked. "'Pay more attention to me'?"

Somehow that made me laugh, and after a moment Anna joined in. Then she leaned over and patted my arm. This time I let her.

"So you forgive me?" she asked.

I nodded. "As long as you forgive me too," I said. "I guess I can be an attention hog."

"And a cookie hog," Anna said with a smile, gesturing down at the empty box in front of me.

I hadn't even realized it, but I'd totally eaten all the cookies! "Sorry!"

Anna jokingly rolled her eyes. "Just like I knew you would," she said.

"I guess I was hungry after than inedible dinner," I said, standing up and rifling through the cabinet. After a moment I pulled out a box of gingersnaps. "These are all yours," I said, handing her the box. "I promise not to eat a single one."

"I think I can share a few," Anna said, opening the box and holding it out to me.

"Maybe just one," I said, and we both laughed again.

But then Anna looked serious. "Is something else going on?" she asked me. "Because it seems like you're upset about more than just me nagging you."

For a moment I wondered if I should tell Anna about Brianna. It was kind of humiliating to admit that someone at school was picking on me. But then I remembered that Anna had just shared a lot with me. And I liked that she trusted me—it was way better than being teased. So maybe it was worth it to try trusting her back.

I poured out the whole story: the things Brianna said, the ways I'd tried to stop her, and how it seemed to be getting worse and worse. Anna listened, nodding in the right places and eating her cookies quietly. When I was done I felt tired but also lighter, the way I had after I'd told Kim and Sasha the whole story.

"That's rough," Anna said sympathetically.

"Yeah," I agreed with a sigh. "And I don't know what to do."

Anna tilted her head thoughtfully. "Why do you

think she does it?" she asked. "I mean, why you out of all the students at your school?"

"I don't know," I said. I'd expected Anna to give me advice, not ask questions.

"Is it a race thing?" she asked.

I shook my head. "I mean, of course I'm not sure, but I don't think so. She's nice to the other black girls in my class. It's just me she hates."

"Or is jealous of," Anna mused.

I suddenly remembered that Kim had said the same thing. "But why would Brianna be jealous of me?" I asked.

Anna shrugged. "That I don't know," she said. "But it's worth thinking about. Because I think the key to getting her to stop picking on you is to figure out why she's doing it in the first place."

I nodded slowly because that really did make sense. "Thanks," I said as we began clearing up the mess from our snacks. "I'm going to think about it."

"If all else fails," Anna said, "let me know and I'll

come take care of her. No one messes with my little sister."

Anna hadn't ever talked to me like this and it made me feel all warm and cozy. I looked at her putting the cookie box away and suddenly, before I'd considered what might happen, I threw my arms around her.

For a moment Anna froze. The two of us never hugged.

But then she wrapped her arms around me and squeezed me tight.

"Thanks, little sister," she said softly into my shoulder. "I really needed that."

"Me too," I said. And it was true.

16

"Wow," Kim said, grinning.

"Taylor, that's awesome," Sasha added happily, reaching across our booth at the Rox to squeeze my hand. I'd just told them the whole story about Anna, and they were as pleased about it as I was.

"Yeah, it's pretty great," I agreed. "It was so nice this morning, just to hang out together and not worry about getting into a fight." Usually I slept in on Saturdays, but this morning I'd gotten up early to cook a big pancake breakfast for my family—they deserved it after the dinner I'd served last night! Anna had complimented my pancakes and I'd made sure not to interrupt when she, Tasha, and Jasmine were discussing the upcoming student council election at the high school. All in all it had been great.

"Here you are, girls," Kim's mom said, setting two baskets of steaming sweet potato fries, the Rox's specialty, down on our table.

"Thanks," we chorused.

"Let me know if you need anything else," she said, blowing us a kiss as she went back to the kitchen. The Rox was bustling with Saturday lunch customers. Already we'd seen Emily and her sister, some friends from Sasha's dance class, and Mrs. Washington, who all stopped by our booth to say hi. One of the things that made Roxbury Park so special was the fact that every time you were out, you ran into friends.

"Your mom's so nice," Sasha said as she picked up a fry and popped it into her mouth.

"And her cooking is the best," I said. Kim's parents both cooked, but it was her mom who came up with most of the recipes. A moment ago I'd been feeling stuffed with pancakes, but the fries smelled so good I suddenly felt my appetite coming back and I grabbed a fry too.

"Anna said something else," I said, remembering that I'd wanted to tell them this part too. "About Brianna."

"Did she have any ideas about how to get her to back off?" Sasha asked, scowling slightly at the mention of Brianna.

"She actually said what you guys did, about Brianna maybe being jealous of me," I said, reaching for a handful of fries. They were good! "And she thought if I could figure out why Brianna's jealous then I could probably figure out how to get her to leave me alone."

Kim nodded thoughtfully. "That makes sense," she said. "So why do you think she's jealous?"

I held out my hands. "No clue," I said. "That's

where I need your help."

We thought about it as we munched our way through the fries. The cheerful sounds of laughter and happy conversation surrounded us, along with the smells of fries, coffee, and apple pie.

"Well, what do we know about Brianna?" Sasha asked, taking a sip of her water and then playing with her straw. "Aside from the fact that she's being really mean right now."

"We know her mom owns Pampered Puppy," Kim said. "So she probably isn't jealous of our Dog Club since she's got her own."

"And she has friends," I added as I wiped my fingers off on a napkin.

Kim's forehead creased. "Who?" she asked.

"I've seen her with a bunch of different people," I said, thinking about it. "Like once I saw her hanging out with Kendra and Meredith. And another time she was with some of the girls in our math class."

"So people like her, but she doesn't have one group

or one best friend," Kim said thoughtfully. "I wonder if that's part of the problem."

"Because you have the two best friends a girl could hope for," Sasha said with a grin.

"Totally," I said. Something else was occurring to me. "Brianna always calls me New Girl, like there's something bad about it," I said slowly. "But wasn't she new last year?"

"Yeah," Kim said. "And now that I think about it, I saw her sitting alone a lot."

Sasha was nodding. "I remember that too," she said. "I once asked her to be partners for an English project because no one else chose her."

It was all starting to come together. "So she had a hard time when she was new," I said.

"And in some ways she probably still feels new," Sasha added. "Since she doesn't have a close group of friends."

"But you came in and everything was great for you: friends, founding a club, fitting in with everybody here," Sasha said.

"Right," I said, starting to feel like we were finally getting to the bottom of things. "I mean, leaving my old friends behind and being the new kid was hard. But to Brianna it must have looked like everything was perfect from the start, which totally wasn't what happened to her."

"So that's why she's jealous," Kim said triumphantly. "You've barely been here at all and your life is awesome, while she still struggles with being new."

"And that probably makes her feel insecure," Sasha said. "Like, why does everyone love you but not her?"

"Obviously it's because I'm fabulous," I joked. But then I got serious. "I think we've figured it out, you guys. I think that's why Brianna's been giving me such a hard time."

Sasha took the last fry. "Yup," she agreed.

"And now that I know what the problem is," I said, "I can finally fix it!"

Sunday I slept late and had a lazy morning. But in the afternoon I finished up the last of my homework and then began going through the photos I'd taken that week at the shelter. We were trying to update the blog more, to keep it interesting, and I wanted to find some fun pictures to post.

Since the dogs were so cute, that was pretty easy. I found a great shot of Boxer and Lily playing dog basketball and I cropped it a little, so you could really see their faces. Boxer's mouth was open in this sweet way that made it look like he was smiling.

The next picture I came to was one of Gus joyfully greeting Mr. Washington. He was jumping up and Mr. Washington was bending down, so their faces were close. They both looked so happy. The next shot was one of Popsicle, Coco, and Gus all racing after a Frisbee, ears flying and faces full of doggy joy.

As I stared at the picture, an idea began to bloom in my mind. I started searching through all my photos, seeking out the ones that showed the dogs at their happiest. If everyone in town could really see how joyful the dogs were during their time at the shelter, there would be no question about how awesome our Dog Club was. *That* was the message we needed to get out there, and fast.

The only question was, How?

17

"You're right," Sasha said as we walked to the shelter after school. We'd already picked up our dogs and had run into each other on Main Street. "If we could get the town to see all those photos, we'd have more clients than we could handle."

Kim was nodding as she pulled gently on Coco's leash to get her to stop while we waited for the light to change. "Those pictures really are worth a thousand words," she agreed. "They say everything we want people to know about our Dog Club. And they say it without being nasty about Pampered Puppy."

"Yeah, I like that part of it too," I admitted. "My dad always calls it mudslinging when politicians start insulting each other, and we don't want to do that. We just want people to know we take awesome care of dogs."

Sasha giggled. "I like the idea of throwing a little mud at Pampered Puppy," she said.

I laughed and poked her. "You know what I mean. We don't want to start some kind of mean back-and-forth. Kim was right before: that's not who we are. Dogs having a great time and getting excited to see their owners—*that's* who we are."

"Hear, hear," Kim applauded happily.

We were passing the Ice Creamery and a couple of girls from our homeroom waved. It was warm and sunny—a good day for ice cream. Gus danced on the end of his leash as we came up to the shelter.

"You're ready to play, aren't you?" I asked him as we walked in.

Tim and Caley called greetings as Kim, Sasha, and I let the club dogs off their leashes and our afternoon at the shelter officially began.

Humphrey headed to his favorite corner for a nap while Popsicle ran to greet Lily and Boxer. Gus went over to a pile of toys on the floor, carefully selected a blue ball, and took it over to Tim. Mr. S ran over to say hi to Caley, who knelt down to hug him, while Coco, Daisy, and Gracie began playing fetch with Kim. It was bustling and happy, but I had to admit it felt a little empty. I missed Hattie—we all did—but it was more than that. The Dog Club really didn't have enough clients, and if we didn't get some new ones soon, it was going to be a problem.

I tossed a tennis ball for Popsicle, Boxer, and Lily, then walked over to Caley. I knew she and Tim cared about the club as much as we did, and maybe they'd have some ideas on how to get our pictures out there.

"I had this thought," I began, "about how we can show people how great our Dog Club is."

"Good," Caley said as she took the soggy tennis ball from Popsicle and sent it back across the room. "Because we really have to do something."

"Yeah," Tim agreed, sounding somber, not like his usual cheerful self.

The thought that Alice wouldn't have the money to take care of the shelter made my chest ache.

"I was thinking—" I began, but then the door opened and Alice walked in.

"Hi," she said. She was wearing her Roxbury Park Dog Club shirt, my very favorite of all her awesome dog tees. Coco, Popsicle, and Gus ran to greet her and she gave them each a warm pat. "How's everybody doing?"

"Taylor was just about to tell us a plan she came up with, to get more customers for the Dog Club," Caley said, brushing back a strand of red hair.

Alice frowned slightly, a sure sign that she was worried about the club and money, which did nothing for the tightness in my chest. But I took a deep breath and told everyone about my idea for a photo montage of dogs playing happily at our Dog Club.

"I love it," Caley declared, clapping her hands together.

"Agreed," Tim said. "It's the perfect way to demonstrate how great the club is."

"Way better than corny ads that have a nasty edge," Caley added. Clearly she'd seen the latest postings from Pampered Puppy.

"The only problem is, where do we put up the pictures?" I asked. Boxer set his Frisbee at my feet and looked up expectantly. I threw it across the room, smiling as he, Lily, and Popsicle raced after it.

"Maybe more flyers?" Caley asked.

"There isn't room for a real montage on a flyer," I said. "Flyers are too small. We want something where people can see a bunch of photos and really get a feel for the club."

"Like a billboard?" Caley asked, frowning. "I don't think we can afford that."

"Too bad we can't do a TV ad," Kim said. She was

now petting Humphrey, who sighed in contentment. "Everyone would see that."

"Or one of those ads they show at the movie theater, before the previews," Sasha said.

"Is there anywhere else a lot of people go, where we could afford to place an ad?" Caley asked.

But no one could think of anything.

"I guess flyers are the only thing we can do," Kim said with a sigh. "Maybe we can print them on bigger paper so we can fit more photos on. And maybe more people will read them this time."

And that was when I came up with the perfect solution. "Everybody reads *Your Roxbury Park*," I said enthusiastically. "I wonder if there's any way we could get the paper to print some of our photos."

Tim frowned. "It's a great idea but it seems like kind of a long shot."

Caley was shaking her head. "I bet they get hundreds of ideas every week since they're so popular."

I felt my spirits sink. But then Alice cleared her

throat. "Actually, thanks to the Dog Club, you guys have a bit of an in at *The Roxbury Park Gazette*."

We all looked at her, confused.

"Mrs. Washington," Alice said with a smile. "Gus's owner. She's the features editor for the paper. And unless I'm very much mistaken, she adores the Dog Club and would be happy to help out."

A current of excitement zipped across the room.

"I so didn't know that," Caley said.

"It's perfect!" Sasha bubbled. Mr. S heard her happiness and pranced over for a hug.

"Do you really think she'll do it?" I asked Alice.

She spread out her hands and smiled. "Only one way to find out," she said, then headed into her office, Oscar at her heels.

"Taylor, you should be the one to ask her," Sasha said immediately.

"Yes," Kim agreed. "They're your pictures and it was your great idea."

Usually I was comfortable talking to anyone, but

this kind of intimidated me. What if I messed it up and ruined our big chance to save our club? "Maybe Caley or Tim should do it," I said.

Caley shook her head. "This is all you, Taylor," she said. "And you're going to totally rock it."

"She said it," Tim added. "You'll be great."

I wasn't so sure, but everyone was clearly decided.

We took the dogs into the backyard for an afternoon of fetch, dog tag, and sun. As always I had a blast with the dogs and my friends, but a corner of my mind was thinking about Mrs. Washington, planning what I would say, what pictures I would show her, and hoping I didn't make a mess of things.

By the time Mrs. Washington arrived, I was ready. I let her greet Gus and then headed over.

"I was hoping I could show you something," I said, holding up my camera. "A picture."

"Sure," she said cheerfully, leaning over to see the image I'd selected. It was from a few weeks ago when she'd been a little late getting Gus. Maybe he'd known because he'd been especially exuberant when she arrived, bounding up to meet her. I'd captured the moment when his feet were off the ground, his face filled with joy as his nose touched her cheek. Mrs. Washington was bending down, beaming, and the whole image had a golden hue from the setting sun shining through the windows.

"Oh, Taylor," Mrs. Washington said as she gazed at the photo. "It's breathtaking. You really are a talented photographer."

I hadn't expected that and for a moment I was too overwhelmed to speak. An actual newspaper editor had called me talented! But then I focused.

"I'm so glad you like it," I said. "Because I was hoping"—I paused to wave my arm toward the others—"we were all hoping that you might consider putting a few of our pictures in *Your Roxbury Park*."

"Oh," she said.

I couldn't read any meaning into that one word so I continued, talking too fast because I was so nervous.

"See, the thing is, there's another doggy day care in town, and we aren't getting any new clients. We were hoping that if we made a montage of photos and it was in *Your Roxbury Park*, people would see and want to sign up for our Dog Club." She didn't say anything, so I went on, babbling now. "The pictures would all be like this—dogs playing and stuff—so people can see how much fun the dogs have at the club."

I stopped because I was out of breath, but still Mrs. Washington stayed silent, absently rubbing Gus's ears.

I glanced back at Sasha and Kim, who both looked confused. Tears pricked my eyes. I'd blown it. I'd said too much or the wrong thing or—

"It's a great idea," Mrs. Washington said, her face breaking into a smile. "I love it."

I was so relieved and happy that I couldn't contain my squeal of joy. Kim, Sasha, Tim, and Caley were cheering, and with all that excitement the dogs went nuts, racing around happily, like it was all a big party. Which it kind of was.

"If you get me the photos by Wednesday, they can be in next Sunday's *Your Roxbury Park*," Mrs. Washington said over the din. "I think my boss will be fine with bumping the fall harvest pictures we'd planned to run until the following week."

I thanked her about fifty times and then let her walk out with Gus.

"You did it," Kim said, throwing her arms around me.

"When people see those pictures, they'll be lining up for our club," Sasha said, wrapping her arms around both of us.

I couldn't stop smiling. "I hope so," I said. "I really hope so."

18

A few days later Kim and I waited at the corner for Sasha.

"She's pushing it," Kim said in a worried voice. "We're going to have to go in a minute."

But just then we saw Sasha racing up the block, backpack thumping on her shoulders as she ran.

"Sorry," she said when she reached us. She was sniffling a little and her eyes were red.

"Sash, what's wrong?" I asked.

"Just my mom," Sasha said, her chin trembling as we started toward school. "She's really mad at me."

Kim and I were on either side of Sasha, leaning in protectively, and we exchanged a glance.

"About the math stuff?" Kim asked gently.

"Yeah," Sasha said. "And she caught me up late last night trying to finish my reading for English."

"Wasn't she glad you were getting it done?" I asked. It seemed like staying up late now and then shouldn't be a big deal if Sasha had work to get done.

"No," Sasha said, chin wobbling. "I mean, she wants me to get it done but she said I need to get it done earlier. But I just can't fit it all in!"

As Sasha rubbed her eyes and Kim gave her a hug, I decided it was time for action. After all, we'd come up with plans to take on Pampered Puppy and Brianna—now we needed to tackle Sasha's schedule. "We are going to fix this," I announced as we stopped for a red light.

"We are?" Sasha asked.

"Yes." I nodded firmly. "There has to be something you can change in your schedule to give you a little more time, and we are going to hunt it down."

Sasha laughed, which made me feel good. At the very least, my plan was cheering her up!

Kim was nodding thoughtfully. "Taylor's right," she said. "We just need to rework your schedule."

"How?" Sasha asked.

"We go through everything you do every day, starting from when you wake up all the way until you go to bed," I said.

"Okay," Sasha said agreeably. "I wake up at six thirty, I walk Mr. S, I shower, I eat, and then I meet you guys. Except I'm always late."

"Maybe you can shower at night?" Kim asked.

"But I don't have time at night either," Sasha said.

"Maybe you should get up earlier," I said.

"But I'm too tired," Sasha moaned. "I usually hit snooze twice before I get up at all."

"Hm, so that means you aren't actually up until

six fifty," I said. We were getting closer to school, and there were groups of kids ahead of us on the sidewalk.

"Oh, I guess that's true," Sasha said, surprised. "I never thought about it, but maybe that's why I don't have enough time. Seriously, though, I'm so tired I can barely drag myself out of bed."

"Okay, so if we figure out how you can get to bed earlier, you'll be able to get up at six thirty and have enough time for everything you need to do in the morning," I said, my feet swishing through a pile of leaves on the sidewalk. I felt like we were making progress, especially when Sasha nodded.

"Okay, so tell us about your afternoons," Kim said.

"I have dance or Dog Club," Sasha said, ticking things off on her fingers. "I get home around six, my mom and I make dinner and clean up. She has a big case, so she usually works in her home office for a few hours while I do homework and walk Mr. S. And then I go to bed."

I considered this. "That shouldn't take so long," I

said. "Are you sure that's all you do?"

"Yeah," Sasha said. "I mean, I do some stuff online, looking at dog blogs and stuff when I take homework breaks."

Kim and I looked at each other. She was raising an eyebrow and I was grinning.

"How long do you read the blogs?" I asked.

Sasha, who hadn't noticed my silent exchange with Kim, twisted a curl as she thought about it. "I don't know, not that long," she said. "There are some really neat videos though. I watched this one last night where an owner was teaching a dog how to ring a bell when the dog wanted to go out. But somehow he taught it wrong and the dog got confused and thought the bell was for when she wanted to eat. So the owner had to totally retrain the dog."

"Sash, that sounds like a pretty long video," I said. "Totally cute, but long."

Sasha blinked and then realization spread across her face. "You know, I think you might be right. Because

I thought I had all this homework time and then suddenly it was ten and I'd barely done anything." She smiled sheepishly. "I also watched this one about a dog whose owner got back from overseas and they had this amazing reunion. I watched it like ten times because it was so sweet."

"Well, that's it," I said as we joined the crowd heading up the path to school. "If you keep your video watching to weekends, you'll have plenty of time to get everything else done."

"And get sleep too," Kim added.

Sasha was beaming as she threw an arm around each of us. "You guys are brilliant," she crowed happily.

"We can't deny it," I joked.

Sasha laughed, but as we walked in the front doors, her face turned serious. "Thanks, you guys," she said. "If this works, and I think it will, you totally saved me."

"From what?" Kim asked, frowning.

"My mom!" Sasha said, laughing again. "She's so irritated she's about to explode! Actually I guess you saved her too, from having a heart attack or something. So thank you!"

"Anytime," I said happily.

One problem down, two more to go. And as I headed to my locker I was sure that we were going to fix them too!

"Watch it, New Girl," Brianna said snidely. The final bell had rung and I was walking toward the front door of the school to meet Kim and Sasha at our usual spot. But the sound of Brianna's voice stopped me in my tracks. Yes, my heart was thumping hard in my chest, but it was time to take care of things with Brianna once and for all.

"It's tough being the new girl, isn't it?" I asked in an even voice, gripping my hands together so she couldn't see them shaking.

Brianna's eyes opened in shock, then narrowed dangerously. "I don't know what you mean," she snapped.

"I'm just saying it's hard starting at a new school," I said, moving to the side of the hall as three boys came racing by. "I know you were new last year and I bet it was even more difficult for you since you didn't know anyone."

Brianna was silent but her face was hard. I pushed on, figuring I'd say all I had to say and hope for the best.

"I mean, I met Sasha over the summer because my dad was friends with her mom," I said. My voice was getting squeaky, so I took a moment to breathe before going on. "And I was so glad to have a familiar face that first day I came here because it's pretty intimidating."

Brianna shrugged. "Not really."

She wasn't giving me anything, but I pushed on. "This school is much bigger than my old one," I said. "That first day I got lost, like, every time we changed classes."

Her face was still set.

"Plus I missed my old friends," I said, starting to wonder if this was going to be another failed attempt. "There's something cool about being with people who knew you when you were five and you shared animal crackers at snack time."

And finally Brianna smiled. It was only there for a second, but I saw it. I watched her start twisting the strap on her bag. "It looked pretty easy for you," she said after a moment, not meeting my eyes.

But my heart jumped anyway. She was actually responding to what I said and not just making fun of me! "I can see how it would look that way," I said, not wanting to disagree and make room for a fight. "But actually Kim and I had big issues at first. And I had a tough time at the dog shelter."

"I thought you loved it there," Brianna said, looking at me without glaring for the first time ever. Her eyes were a warm shade of brown.

"I do now," I said. "But at first I was scared of the big dogs. And that made me a total third wheel. Everyone was having this great time playing, while I was terrified of getting attacked."

Brianna laughed. She actually laughed at my joke.

"So yeah, it probably looked like coming here was totally easy for me," I said, brushing a stray braid out of my face. "But it was harder than it looked."

"But you're happy now," Brianna said, a trace of wistfulness in her voice. "You have this great group of friends, and everyone likes you."

My friends had called it: Brianna was jealous of me. And truthfully I could understand why. My life here was pretty great.

"I am happy," I said. "But I've also worked hard to make Roxbury Park my home."

Brianna nodded thoughtfully at that.

"I still miss my old friends," I went on. I wanted her to know that even though I was happy, my life wasn't perfect. "And I'm still getting used to certain things here. I think the winters are going to be a real trial for this Southern girl."

Brianna smiled again.

"You know, if you ever want to stop making fun of me and start hanging out, you could sit with us at lunch sometime," I said, taking the final leap. The halls had pretty much emptied out, and I could see the janitor sweeping. We were going to have to get going soon. "Kim and Sasha are nice—you'd like them."

Brianna looked sheepish. "You'd really want to be friends with me," she asked, "after I've been kind of obnoxious?"

I raised an eyebrow and planted a hand on my hip.

Brianna laughed. "Okay, more than kind of. I've been obnoxious and I'm sorry. And if you're serious, I'd like to join you guys one day."

"Okay then," I said, smiling.

"See you tomorrow," Brianna said, almost shyly. She was smiling, too, as she headed toward the library

I headed for the door. I was late but I knew my friends wouldn't be mad at me, not when they heard my news! In fact, as I pushed through the heavy front door and out into the sunny afternoon, I decided we were going to stop at the Ice Creamery.

Because with their help and Anna's, I'd just turned an enemy into a friend—and that was worth celebrating!

19

My friends had been thrilled when
I filled them in on the latest with
Brianna. And after dinner I'd told
Anna the whole story, and she was
so proud she squealed. Which was
pretty great.

Now I was up in my room, putting together the
photo montage for *Your Roxbury Park*. Our parents had
agreed that I could use a few pictures of us in addition to the dogs and their owners, since the paper was

local. We were all pretty excited to get our pictures in *Your Roxbury Park* but even more excited that now people could see how much fun the dogs had with us. We might not be "professionals," but you could see in the pictures how much we loved the dogs. And how much the dogs loved us!

I started with the picture of Mrs. Washington and Gus, then scrolled through some of the other shots. I added one of Boxer, Humphrey, and Lily all sitting on Kim's lap, then one of Sasha, Tim, and Caley running with Popsicle, Gus, Coco, and Mr. S. You could see the joy on the dogs' faces, and Sasha, Tim, and Caley were all laughing happily. I scrolled through a few more and then my breath caught as I came to a shot of Ms. Wong bending down to snuggle Hattie. At first all I could see was our beloved Hattie, who we all missed. But then I began to look at the photo more closely.

Ms. Wong was smiling, her cheek pressed against Hattie's fur. She couldn't see Hattie's face but I could, and Hattie was the picture of bliss, cuddled against Ms.

Wong. Just a quick glance told you that Hattie knew exactly who her owner was and where she belonged. As I stared at the photo the love between owner and pup so obvious it radiated, something occurred to me. Maybe, just maybe, if the Wongs could see actual evidence of Hattie's love for them, even when she was at the shelter, they'd reconsider and let her come back to the Dog Club.

So at the end of the night, when I had all my pictures laid out perfectly, that one was front and center. I saved the document, then sent it to Mrs. Washington, fingers crossed that this would be what finally got our Dog Club the customers we needed to keep the shelter open.

The next day I saw Brianna in the locker alcove. My shoulders automatically scrunched up, but then I remembered: we were okay now. At least I hoped we were.

Then Brianna turned, caught my eye, and smiled. Yeah, we were okay.

I couldn't stop grinning as I twirled my locker combination.

It felt kind of funny to be walking over to our lunch table with Brianna right behind me, smiling instead of glaring. Emily, Rachel, Naomi, and Dana all did a double take when they saw her. But then they greeted her and passed us a Tupperware of cookies that Naomi and her mom had baked. They were shortbread with a layer of caramel topped with chocolate sprinkles.

"Wow, I'm sitting with you guys every day if you always eat like this," Brianna said after biting into her first one.

"Yeah, we all stuff ourselves when Naomi brings in cookies," Kim said, her mouth full. "She and her mom should open a bakery."

"Seriously," I agreed, taking another one.

Brianna cleared her throat. "So, I know you guys have seen some of the ads my mom ran for Pampered Puppy," she said, her cheeks turning red. "My mom can be a little, um, aggressive and she's really excited about doing the doggy day care."

"Yeah, we kind of got that," Sasha said in a neutral voice, nibbling on a cookie as she waited to hear what Brianna would say next.

"Last night, after Taylor invited me to sit with you guys and stuff, I had a talk with her," Brianna went on. "She agreed to tone down the ads."

Kim, Sasha, and I beamed at each other, then at Brianna.

"That's awesome; thanks," I said.

"Well, I figure there are enough dogs in Roxbury Park for two doggy day cares," she said. Then she lowered her voice and looked just at me. "And I figured I owed you one."

"Thanks," I said. "That means a lot."

"And by the way," she added with a grin, "I love your shirt—that color is great on you. I may just have to find one like it for myself."

I looked down at my pink shirt and burst out laughing.

★ ★ ★

I was so excited about our Dog Club being featured in *Your Roxbury Park* that I could barely sleep on Saturday night. On Sunday morning I was up with the sun, which was more than a little unusual, and the second my eyes opened I leaped out of bed and rushed downstairs. A wet, chilly breeze blew into the front hall when I opened the door, but *The Roxbury Park Gazette* was sitting on the porch, already waiting for me.

I grabbed it, ran into the kitchen, and shuffled through the sections of the newspaper until my fingers touched the sleek pages of the Sunday magazine. I pulled *Your Roxbury Park* out and then let out a gasp when I saw the cover. THE ROXBURY PARK DOG CLUB it said in big letters. There was a picture of me, Kim, and Sasha surrounded by club and shelter dogs, the three of us grinning. I hadn't taken that shot but I remembered who had: Alice. Apparently I wasn't the only one sending photos to Mrs. Washington!

For a moment I just gazed down at it. Who'd have thought I'd ever be on the front of a magazine like this! But finally I flipped it open, and for a second time my breath caught in my chest. The photo spread was amazing. I mean, maybe as the photographer it was boasting to say it, but there was something about seeing the club pictures all blown up and perfectly airbrushed that made them look incredible. I paged through, admiring the work Mrs. Washington and the other editors had done. There were quotes from the website mixed in with the photos, as well as a short history of the club that described Kim, Sasha, and me as "true dog lovers and a real credit to the Roxbury Park community." I couldn't wait to show my dad that! And at the bottom was all the info needed for anyone to sign up for our Dog Club. In a word, it was perfect. Absolutely perfect.

"Can I see?" Anna asked, coming into the kitchen. Jasmine and Tasha were right behind her. All three of my sisters looked sleepy, and I realized they'd gotten up early to see this. My heart swelled as I stepped back so they could take a look.

"This is fantastic!" Anna crowed when she saw the cover.

The three of them turned the pages slowly, shrieking in excitement over every detail.

"What's all the noise?" Dad asked.

For a second I worried we'd disturbed him since Dad loved sleeping in, but then I saw that he was smiling as he slipped on his reading glasses. "Let's see what the fuss is about."

My sisters moved over, and soon my whole family was exclaiming about my pictures, my Dog Club, my friends, and me.

"I feel like I'm the sister of a celebrity," Tasha said proudly. "I'm bringing this to show off at work today." She had a part-time job at the Roxbury Park Cineplex.

"Wait, I want to bring it to Sugar and Spice to show everyone on my afternoon shift." Jasmine pouted. Sugar and Spice was the candy store on Main Street where she worked on weekends.

"Not to worry," Dad said. "I plan on buying about

a hundred of these. After all, we have a lot of relatives who are going to want to see what a great thing Taylor has done here."

Joy was bubbling up in me, fizzy and sweet, and I couldn't stop smiling.

Anna wrapped an arm around me. "I'm going to cook a big brunch to celebrate," she announced.

I might have burst into tears of joy right then if the phone hadn't started ringing.

"It's me," Sasha said when I picked up, her voice giddy. "Alice just sent me two calls and three emails from potential clients. Your photos did it, Taylor. The Roxbury Park Dog Club is back in business!"

"Two points and the game is ours!" I shouted, raising my arms over my head the way Tim always did. Gus had just taken the winning shot in our game of doggy basketball and we were the champs, at least for this round.

Tim, the opposing coach, scowled. "I think there

should have been a foul called on Lily when she jumped into the basket," he said. "That totally messed up Popsicle's shot."

I laughed. "You're a sore loser," I told him playfully, and now he laughed.

"It's called a winning spirit," he told me. Coco brought over a Frisbee, which he threw across the room. Coco, Boxer, Lily, and Mr. S took off after it. I headed over to the corner, where Humphrey was snuggling with Sasha, who was on the phone.

"Okay, we'll let you know just as soon as we can schedule that first visit with you," Sasha said, her voice professional. But when she hung up she pretended to faint. "That was, like, my fiftieth call today. I'm never going to get to play with the dogs!" But she was grinning.

After just a few days, Sasha reported that cutting out her video time had made a huge difference. She was able to do everything she needed to and get to bed on time, and didn't even need to press snooze on her alarm because she was no longer exhausted when it went off.

"I can't wait to meet some new dogs," Kim said cheerfully. She was giving Gracie a tummy rub.

We'd had so many calls and emails that we'd had to start a wait list. Which was pretty great. We had three potential new dogs that would be coming in for a first meeting next week. And if all went well, our club would be full again!

"I wonder if we should refer some of the calls to Pampered Puppy," Kim said thoughtfully.

"No way," Tim said. He was still playing Frisbee with Coco, Popsicle, and Lily, but Mr. S was taking a break to come cuddle with Humphrey, while Boxer had joined the Frisbee game.

"Tim, be nice," Caley fake scolded, a hand on her hip. But then she looked at Kim. "He does have a point though. Why would we help them?"

"It's to help the dogs and their owners," I said, knowing just why Kim had suggested it. "If we don't have room, the dogs should still have a fun place to go in the afternoon."

"And maybe if we give them some referrals now, they'll give some back to us if we need them later," Sasha said, her business sense coming out.

"I doubt it," Caley said, wrinkling her nose. She leaned over to pet Gus, who leaned against her leg.

"Stranger things have happened though," I said, thinking of Brianna. She'd asked me to be her partner for the math project we were doing in class, and so far it was going great.

I was about to suggest that we take the dogs out back when the front door opened. We all looked to see who it was, and a moment later a big white ball of fluff streaked in.

"Hattie!" I cried as we all ran over to greet her.

The dogs came too, so Hattie, who was running in joyful circles, was immediately surrounded by people petting her and dogs coming up for a good sniff. When she came to me, I bent down and gave her a big hug.

She panted happily in my ear, then gave me a lick on the face and moved on to greet Sasha, who was nearly tearful with joy.

Ms. Wong stood in doorway, smiling as Hattie made her rounds. Alice had come out of her office and after she gave Hattie a loving pat, she turned to Ms. Wong.

"How's Hattie doing these days?" Alice asked, smoothing back a strand of hair that had fallen out of her ponytail.

"She's great," Ms. Wong said proudly. "We've been working on training her, and she's very obedient now. She always comes when we call her and she's getting much better at sitting. And really, she's such a sweetheart." She gazed lovingly at Hattie, but then looked back at Alice. "There's just one problem."

Kim, Sasha, and I glanced at each other, worried.

"Is it something we can help with?" Alice asked.

"Yes," Ms. Wong said. "Hattie misses coming here, and we're hoping you'll have her back in the Dog Club."

Kim, Sasha, Tim, Caley, and I all cheered, which

made the dogs go bonkers with excitement.

Alice was laughing. "I think you can take that as a yes," she said.

"Great," Ms. Wong said with a grin, reaching into her purse and pulling out her house key. "You can pick her up for the next meeting."

"But you're not taking her now, are you?" I asked.

Ms. Wong laughed, then gestured to where Hattie was playing fetch with Kim, Boxer, and Lily. "How could I?" she asked.

"I'm so glad you changed your mind," Alice said as she walked Ms. Wong back toward the door.

"Actually, it was the picture in *Your Roxbury Park* that did it," Ms. Wong said. "The one of me and Hattie. I could see we'd made a mistake, that she was happy at the club but she knew we were her people."

"Yeah, she's smart like that," I said, snuggling Hattie, who had come over. I buried my face in her fur, thrilled that my plan to get her back had worked.

"We overreacted," Ms. Wong said, "being new

owners and all. But we're figuring it out. And we know she'll be happy here."

She waved and then headed for the door.

"I'm so glad Hattie's back," Sasha said with a happy sigh.

"With Hattie and all the new dogs who want to join the club, we are in great shape," Caley said.

Alice nodded. "We sure are," she said. "Thanks to your photos, Taylor, and the hard work all of you do around here."

Hearing that made me start beaming all over again. All of us were; Alice didn't give praise unless she really meant it.

"You know what it's time for," Tim said, grabbing the laundry basket. "I'm mounting a comeback, and Hattie's going to be my star forward."

"You're on," I said. Kim and Sasha came over to help me get our team ready, while Caley walked over to Tim.

"We're winning this one for sure," Sasha told them tauntingly.

"I don't think so," Caley taunted back, laughing. "This one's ours."

But as we began our rousing game, everyone laughing and joking as we ran around, I knew that really we were all the winners. Our club was in great shape, Brianna was becoming a friend, Hattie was back, and, most important of all, we had each other.

And there was nothing better than that.

DON'T MISS THE NEXT DOG CLUB ADVENTURE!

Kim may be Roxbury Park's dog whisperer, but between trouble with schoolwork and a challenging new member of the Dog Club, she has her work cut out for her—and she'll need a helping hand (or paw) from all of her friends!

1

"I've graded your tests," my English teacher, Mrs. Benson, said crisply. The bell for first period had barely finished ringing but she was already starting class and everyone, even Dennis Cartwright, class trouble-maker, was sitting down quietly. Mrs. Benson had that effect on people. It wasn't like she yelled or made scary threats. She just had this look that made you want to do your very best for her.

Which was why I was biting my lip as she began

1

passing back our papers. I really *had* done the best I could. But we'd just finished a biography of Marie Curie and even though it was pretty interesting, I'd gotten a little confused during Mrs. Benson's lectures about it. I'd try to take notes but she talked so fast that I'd still be writing down the first thing she said while she was already onto a whole other subject. And then I'd be so lost I wouldn't know what to write. My notebook was a mess of scribbles that didn't even make sense. Plus sometimes the book got a little confusing. Which was why I'd probably done pretty badly on this test. And that was not going to make my parents happy at all.

Mrs. Benson set a paper in front of my best friend Sasha, who looked at it and grinned. It wasn't so long ago that Sasha was the one having trouble with her home-work, but not because she didn't understand it. She'd just gotten so busy with the Dog Club we'd started, and the dance classes she took after school—plus the new dog she'd adopted from the shelter where we had the club. But Taylor, our other best friend, and I had helped

Sasha figure out how to manage her time a little better and judging from the expression on Sasha's face, it was definitely working.

I saw Taylor give Sasha a small thumbs-up, so she must have noticed too. Then both of them looked at me just as Mrs. Benson put my paper on my desk. She'd set it upside down and just seeing that made my stomach twist. Good grades came face up. I took a breath and turned the paper over slowly. A bright red 68 was scrawled at the top.

My face felt hot and my eyes prickled. My parents had told me how important that test was and I'd promised them I'd study every night. And I had. But I'd still done terribly.

"It's okay, Kim," Sasha whispered sympathetically. Only the best of friends would risk a Mrs. Benson look by talking in class.

I tried to smile at Sasha but the corners of my mouth wouldn't cooperate. The red 68 made smiling impossible.

"So that concludes our unit on biographies," Mrs. Benson said. She was back at the front of the room, her hand resting on the pile of books on her desk. "And now we move on to one of my very favorite books, *The Adventures of Tom Sawyer*. Kwan, Danny, and Taylor, would you please help me pass these out?"

When Taylor set the book on my desk she reached over and squeezed my arm. The beads at the ends of her braids clinked gently as she moved down the aisle, and my skin still felt warm where she'd touched me. The 68 still ate at me but it helped to have Taylor and Sasha.

So I did the only thing I could. I opened my notebook and got ready to write down everything Mrs. Benson had to say about *Tom Sawyer*.

As soon as the bell rang Taylor and Sasha came over to me.

"Don't worry, you'll do better on the next one," Sasha said, pushing a dark brown curl out of her face. Sasha usually wore her hair back in a ballet bun or ponytail, but curls were always springing free as if they had a life of their own.

"Yeah, it's just one test," Taylor added. She was wearing a bright pink T-shirt that made her dark brown skin glow.

"I wish my parents thought that," I said as we headed into the crowded hallway.